For Chris,
my guiding star

The
Island

1

NORTH OF Boston in the Massachusetts Bay is an island shaped like a crescent moon, now joined to the mainland by a man-made causeway. I suppose that means it's not an island anymore. But when I lived there, I always thought of it as an island because many strange and wonderful things happened that can only happen in isolated places. It was the sea that nurtured me there for many years, but it was the causeway that became my lifeline.

Daddy, Mum, Chantel, and I lived in a tiny apartment over our grocery store, The Coop. The Post Office and Ralph's Hardware were next to us on one side. On the other side was Julio's Fish Market which sent the pungent, often rank odor of cod and shellfish drifting down the street.

None of the narrow storefronts had been painted in years, giving them a dingy, weathered look. Mum often talked about painting the shabby green awning and door of our store fire engine red. It was the English love of color coming out in her. But with all the work she had to do, she never got around to it.

From the large picture window in our living room, you could see the Cove at the bottom of the hill. The Cove stretched out towards Boston Harbor. Beyond that was the ocean and nothing else until you came to England where Mum was from. She'd met Daddy there during World War II when she was only sixteen. She ran away to marry him and never went back.

If you kept going, beyond England, you'd eventually get to China, and then Viet Nam. Bobby Muscovi's dad was there.

I would often close my eyes and try to imagine Bobby's dad

flying his helicopter. I would picture him landing in the jungle and being shot at, but then escaping again with a load of wounded soldiers. And I'd pray. Mum said if you believed, God would answer your prayers.

I was doing it at the breakfast table, leaning back with my eyes closed and taking my time chewing on a sausage. Chantel was whining again about having to work in the store, which wasn't helping my concentration much.

"But I need you in the store, Chantel," Mum argued.

"But I can make a lot more money baby-sitting. Janet and I would be partners."

"Janet?" Daddy interrupted. "Isn't she the one who caught the Evans's kitchen on fire?"

"That was an *accident!* Pulleeeeze, Mother, I hate the store. Let Evie do it. She's the one who's crazy about it."

"Evie's too young. She already helps me clean. That's enough."

"What's she doin'?" Daddy growled. I could feel my hair begin to prickle.

"Oh, she's gone into her trance again," Chantel said matter-of-factly.

"What trance?"

"She's meditating. She's always doing it in bed. Whenever I try to talk to her at night, she says, 'Don't bother me, I'm meditating.' It's her way of ignoring us."

"Barbara Eve, finish your breakfast," Mum ordered, tapping me on the shoulder.

"Meditating?" Daddy growled again. "So, when did this start?"

"Ever since Bobby's dad went to Viet Nam." Chantel was always eager to be a source of information.

"Hey! You with your eyes closed!" Daddy snapped. "Don't you have any other friends?"

I flipped my eyes open angrily. Chantel was grinning at me over her glass of milk. Chantel could infuriate me beyond reason. She was fifteen, but tried to look and act like she was twenty. Daddy wouldn't let her date, so she sneaked out at night.

I was threatened with death by slow torture if I ever ratted on her.

"Bobby's my best friend," I said defensively.

"She's too young to . . . to go running around with a boy all the time," Daddy said to Mum. "Particularly this one. He's giving her crazy ideas, spooking her with all kinds of war stories probably."

"You were in a war," I reminded him.

"Yeah, well, this is different, what I'm talking about. Boys and war, it gets them all excited." Daddy reverted back to Mum. "She's eleven. That's when it starts."

"When what starts?" I demanded.

"You start getting ideas about boys."

"I told you, Bobby's my best friend. I don't have any *ideas* about him."

"I mean ideas about wanting to go with them."

"Go where?" I said, slumping in my seat and folding my arms.

"Now, don't you get sarcastic with me, young lady," Daddy threatened with his finger jabbing across the table.

Chantel set down her glass and began twining her dark, glossy hair around her fingers. It was long and thick, and she liked to wear it brushed forward so the ends curled just slightly over her breasts.

"Daddy thinks Bobby's your boyfriend," she giggled.

"He's *not* my boyfriend! How many of your friends have dads in Viet Nam? Huh? You wouldn't care if they did!" I wrapped up my toast in a napkin and shoved back from the table.

"Where you goin' with that?" Daddy demanded.

"I'm gonna feed it to the sea gulls. I'm not hungry anymore. Can I be excused? I have chores to do."

"Yes, you can go," Mum said, quietly sipping her tea. Then, as I stomped out of the room, I heard her say to Daddy, "Why must you talk to her like that? She's just a child."

I turned the vacuum cleaner on high and stormed through the apartment, drowning out all further conversation. Saturday chores were the best excuse ever invented for getting away from the breakfast table. Nobody could ever quarrel with you about wanting to get chores done. Some chores were better than others. Vacuuming was the best because nobody could complain you were making too much noise. It worked all the anger out of you. Not like dusting. With dusting, you had to be careful not to break things. But it was Chantel's turn to dust today.

I flicked off the vacuum, and then headed wordlessly out the door and pounded down the stairs. After unlocking the store, I switched on the lights and revolving overhead fan, grabbed the broom from the back closet, and began attacking the floor. Mum couldn't stand the slightest speck of dirt anywhere, but especially in her store. She wanted it swept morning and evening and then morning again in case I'd missed something.

Everything in The Coop had to be perfect according to Mum. All the cereal, bread, and baking things were arranged in perfect rows on shelves in the center of the store. Canned goods were stacked neatly along the walls. The dairy and freezer section hummed invitingly in the back behind gleaming sliding glass doors. Then there was always some fruit and lettuce, if it was good, in the window because Mum thought fresh produce was what made a store attractive.

In the front next to the cash register was a rack of candy and cigarettes and the coffee bar with three swiveling stools. Mum always had a fresh pot of coffee on so people would hang around a bit to talk and give her company.

Mum ran the grocery store because Daddy had a bad heart and couldn't work. Shed made a success out of it while he kept the books, worked crossword puzzles, and watched television. He never went out and was a grump most of the time. Once, when he'd been with the Coast Guard, he'd been as full of salt and life as the sea itself. He loved it when Mum brought Chantel and me all dressed up in twin dresses to the station. I didn't think he loved us anymore, but Mum hung onto the past.

I swept hard and furiously and began to whistle. Whistling was Mum's way of getting the anger out. "Try whistling, dear," was always her advice when I had a mind to kill Chantel. "That's what I used to do when I was a girl. You can't be angry and whistle at the same time."

I'd start whistling then, until Chantel was ready to slap me. After that, I wasn't angry anymore because I'd gotten her goat.

I heard Mum's firm, even step outside on the stairs and quickly threw the broom back in the closet. She was going to come down and start talking about Daddy, but that morning I didn't want to talk about Daddy. I slipped through the front door, making the little silver bells tinkle overhead, and ran out into the bright, hot September day without looking back.

Bobby Muscovi's house was at the bottom of the hill facing the Cove. "Musk Cove" we called it. There was a small marina of fishing boats at one end and a rocky overhang at the other called Bracken's Hill. As I came running down the stone steps onto the smooth part of the beach, I saw Bobby at the other end near the rocks where he kept his dinghy. He stood up and waved excitedly. Something white fluttered in his hand.

"Hey!" he yelled, his brown face flushed with heat and excitement. "I got a letter from my dad."

I sprinted towards him. "What does it say?" I said breathlessly, peering at it over his shoulder.

"'Dear Bobby,'" he began, his eyes squinting against the light.

How are you, Captain? Taking good care of your mother and Teeny for me, I hope. I shouldn't say hope, but know, because I know you're the best son a father ever had, and the most capable. You'll make the best pilot or ball player or scientist or all three. Which reminds me, how about them Red Sox! Looks as if they're headed for the World Series! It's too much for a man to bear, even for his country and family that he misses and loves so much.

There's been a lot of action here lately. Today our chopper made several trips into a rice paddy to rescue wounded. These Viet Cong seem to come out of nowhere. They've got miles and miles of underground tunnels that keep coughing them up. It seems hopeless at times.

Guess what? We have a little mascot who goes on all our rescue missions! His name is Peanut Brittle because I found him in my bunk devouring the peanut brittle you sent me. He's a chipmunk! I put him in my shirt pocket every day and away we go. He loves the ride.

I know this all sounds exciting to you, but believe me, it's no picnic. This is no place for any human being to be. It's hot and miserable most of the time, with casualties every day. I guess lately I've been wondering why I'm here. I can't wait to be back home with you and Mom and Teeny.

Well, Capt., I'm pretty exhausted. Be my man and love your mother and Teeny ever so tenderly for me. Keep me posted about the Sox!

Love, your Dad

Bobby carefully folded his letter and put it in his pocket. "I sure miss him," he sighed. "I wish he'd hurry up and get home. Mom cries every night after we've gone to bed. I know she thinks we don't hear, but I do." Then, brightening, he gave me a full smile and brushed away the dark hair that was always falling in his eyes. "But at least he's not wounded or anything. He helped rescue all those men. I'll bet he gets a hundred Silver Stars!"

"What's a Silver Star?"

"It's the medal you get for being a hero."

"I wonder if my dad ever won a Silver Star," I said wistfully. "He fought in World War II, you know."

"You should ask him. Maybe he's a hero, and you don't even know it."

"Naw. He doesn't like to talk about war."

"Your mom might know."

I shrugged. "It doesn't really matter."

Bobby squatted down next to a hole he'd been digging in the wet sand. He had a clam rake in one hand and a squirming coffee can in the other. Sea worms. They were horrible, crawly looking things you could actually stretch like a rubber band. It was the only part of fishing I didn't like.

"The Sox are gonna win the pennant, and my dad's missing out," Bobby sighed, pulling a ten-incher out of its hole.

"That's disgusting!" I exclaimed, crinkling up my nose.

Bobby wriggled it at me. "Here, eat it!"

"You eat it!"

"I guess this one could catch a whale," Bobby laughed, dropping it into the can.

"That's what I'm gonna do my science project on, I decided."

"On sea worms!"

"No, Goofus. On whales."

"How come whales?"

"I don't know. I guess I think they're interesting."

"I don't know what I'm going to do mine on," Bobby said thoughtfully. "I'm interested in too many things."

"You'll have the best report as usual," I teased. After all, Bobby was the brain of the class.

I found a stick and lazily began scrawling my name in the sand. "Aren't you glad we finally have Mr. Hughes?"

"I'll say! I like having a guy for a teacher. He doesn't yell at us. Plus, he knows a lot."

Everybody liked Mr. Hughes. After spending six years of my life with crabby old ladies, having Mr. Hughes was as exciting and refreshing as the first day of summer. He told funny stories and invented games and had a desk full of colored chalk he drew pictures with on the chalkboard.

Each week, he said, he'd draw us a different picture. For the first week of school, he'd drawn a swirling blue and green ocean with an old sailing clipper on it and talked about how science has changed things in the world today. He meant sailing ships, but I was thinking about the jewel-colored ocean he'd drawn. I copied his effortless swirls in my notebook, adding a fish here and there, and that's when I began thinking about whales and teaching. Mr. Hughes made teaching and learning seem like a lot of fun even if he did give us a lot of homework.

"That should be enough," Bobby said, shaking the coffee can under my nose.

Squealing, I threw my stick at him. Then he chased me over

to the dinghy. It was an ugly, rough little boat. Once it had been painted red, but the paint was mostly chipped off by now. Bobby said he was waiting to paint it in the spring when his dad came home.

Eagerly, we dragged it down to the water, its bottom scraping against the colored stones that covered half the beachfront. Glistening purple and blue, they reflected the sharp, running sparks of light on the water, and when the waves ran swiftly up over them and back, they made the sound of leaves clapping in a breeze. They were magic because if you took any home with you and put them on a shelf, the next day they would be dull and colorless.

As we rowed, the waves slapped peacefully against the boat, and I felt good again. I was glad that Mr. Hughes was the favorite teacher at Hawthorne School and that I knew what my science project would be. But being here in Musk Cove in a boat with Bobby, that was the best of all.

Bobby baited the hooks on our droplines. Then we tied them to the oar rests, one on each side. We usually caught tinker mackerels or pollack, flounder if we were lucky, and a lot of crabs and riffraff that hung around the lobster traps. Their bright red buoys bobbed up and down at the mouth of the Cove like a scattered string of beads. We never kept anything we caught. It was just for fun.

A gull screeched overhead and put down his landing gear. I carefully unfolded my napkin, now full of crumbs, and lifted up a small piece of crust. Hovering just within reach, he snatched it up and wheeled away, only to circle back for more. Soon, another gull began closing in.

I laughed. "Do you think that's his wife? Every time he comes around, she does, too."

"How do you know it's a she?" Bobby questioned. "Maybe it's his kid brother hanging around and driving him nuts."

"I don't know. It's just this look about her. Here." I handed Bobby half the bread.

"I guess whoever starts laying the eggs, they figure that's the girl gull. Gool gullallall." Bobby began gargling at the female who totally ignored him.

I laughed and flicked water at him. "You weirdo! Do you think we all look alike to them?"

"Probably."

I reluctantly gave up my last crumb. The gulls cocked their heads suspiciously. "All gone," I apologized, holding out empty hands. They lingered a few seconds longer, then sailed high out over the water.

The sun was only halfway towards its zenith, yet already prominent and hot. It was too hot for September. Bobby took his shirt off and stretched back in the dinghy.

I stared at him for a few minutes and wondered if I had any ideas about him. How could you tell?

"Bobby, this is a weird question," I said, curving my hand through the water.

"What weird question?"

"Well, I haven't asked you it yet. But it's weird, so I'm telling you beforehand."

I waited for him to say something, but he closed his eyes instead, which was his way of listening sometimes.

"Okay," I persisted, taking a deep breath. "What I want to know is, are you my boyfriend?"

His eyes fluttered open. Sitting up, he checked his line. "I guess so," he answered thoughtfully. "I don't like any other girls I know, that's for sure, except my mom and sometimes Teeny, but they don't count, I guess."

"Well, have you ever *kissed* anybody, then?" My heart suddenly began pounding like a drum. I'd never said *kiss* in front of a boy before.

"No." He squinted his eyes against the sun and looked at me. "Have you?"

"No."

The sun sparkled lively in the water and winked off the masts of the fishing boats. I leaned far over the side of the dinghy and carved patterns through the waves with my fingers.

"Do you want to?" I said finally.

"Sure."

He was shrugging and grinning with embarrassment. I giggled.

"But what if somebody sees us?"

"We can row behind the hill," Bobby suggested. "We're not catching anything here anyways."

We pulled in our lines. Then Bobby rowed farther out around Bracken's Hill. I nestled back in the dinghy and stared up at the cloudless sky. We rocked quietly for a few minutes. Bobby nervously turned to watch a plane taking off over the harbor. We both watched it make its smooth arc across the sky, climbing and climbing until it was only a speck in the distance.

"Do you want to now?" Bobby said.

"Okay."

He leaned forward shyly, bracing his arms against the oars. With a slight tremble, he kissed me softly on the mouth.

It seemed a strange thing to do. I pulled back, feeling silly and awkward and not any differently toward Bobby. He was still Bobby, short and pudgy with a shy grin on his face.

"Well," he said, breathing. "Now we've kissed."

"My sister has so many boyfriends, she kisses all of them," I blurted. "She sleeps with them, too."

Bobby took this in gravely. Then he readjusted his dropline. Sensing a mistake, I leaned over and cupped my chin in my hands. "I shouldn't have told you. She'd kill me if she ever found out I told anybody. She always brags about it to me and tells me if I ever tell, she'll kill me."

"You should tell her to keep her mouth shut."

I shook my head. "It doesn't do any good. I'll sure never be like her though."

Bobby's shoulders relaxed as if the mistake was over. "I like you, Eve. I hope you're never like that."

Something tugged on my line. Gratefully, I grabbed for it, letting it dance through the water, then come up slowly, wriggling and flapping flashes of silver in the sunlight.

"It's a runt!" Bobby exclaimed, falling back with laughter at my eagerness.

But I didn't care. Everything in the ocean was a wonder to me. I admired the tiny mackerel's beauty a second longer, its desperateness to live. Then I cut it loose and tossed it back.

"Enjoy your breakfast!" I shouted. "Sorry for the inconvenience!" It always seemed the right thing to apologize. Not that it really mattered to the fish. But to nature it might. To God it might. Bobby was Catholic, and Catholics had a long list of things you always had to be saying you were sorry for. We were Episcopalians, which was close to being Catholic.

"Kissing isn't a sin, is it, Bobby?" I asked.

He was at the oars, rowing back towards the marina. Blushing, he looked away. "Kissing isn't a sin, Eve."

We resettled our lines and caught a few more mackerels. "Sorry for the inconvenience!" Bobby yelled as we threw each one back.

"*Sorry for the inconvenience!*" I yelled even louder.

The sun was directly overhead, and we were getting giddy. Bobby stood up in the boat and cupped his hands to his mouth as if he wanted to shout it to the universe and God and everybody. "SORRY FOR THE INCONVENIENCE!"

Laughing hilariously, I stood up to join him. It didn't matter that the dinghy was tipping precariously. Perhaps it was what we both intended. A sailboat was gliding in behind us.

"SORRY FOR THE INCONVENIENCE!" we shouted to the people on the boat.

Then we capsized. Bobby dove in headfirst, and I flew over the side backwards. The water came like an electric shock. Exhilarated, I paddled after the oars, then back towards the overturned dinghy. Bobby was already there, waving the sailboat over.

It came towards us like a giant, elegant butterfly, its sails puffed proudly with the adventure of the day. A woman leaned far over the side and reached towards Bobby.

"Can you give us a ride in?" Bobby asked.

"Sure. Climb aboard," the woman said.

Her husband pulled Bobby in, then me. We flipped over the dinghy and tied it to the back of the sailboat.

"What were you yelling about?" the husband asked.

"Nothing," Bobby said impishly. We looked at each other and giggled.

"It's a beautiful day, isn't it?" the woman remarked, stretching her long, slim arms over her head like a ballerina. "I was just telling my husband it's the most beautiful day of the year. We waited an entire summer for this day."

"Thanks for picking us up," Bobby said. "Actually, we were just being careless."

"Well, it's the most beautiful day of the year, isn't it, Harold?" the woman said, suddenly stretching out her arm and pointing again like a ballerina. "Look, what's that flashing light?"

It was coming from Bobby's back porch. It was Nita signaling us in.

"That's my mom," Bobby explained. "It's lunchtime."

"Is that how she always gets your attention?" the woman asked, incredulous.

"It's the Morse Code. We learned it from my dad. He's a reserve Marine officer in Viet Nam right now."

"Oh, really?" said Harold, clearly impressed.

"Yeah, he's a helicopter pilot. He flies in and rescues the men that get wounded."

"Serious job."

"Yeah. He wanted to do it. He didn't have to, but he wanted to."

"Would you like to flash a message back?" Harold disappeared below deck for a moment and returned with a high-beam flashlight.

"Great!" Bobby said excitedly. "She'll love this." He aimed the flashlight towards home and began flashing. I watched him with admiration. He'd begun teaching me the Code so we could send secret messages at night up and down the hill.

We waited a few moments, and then the light flashed back from shore that the message was received. Harold and his ballerina wife were even more impressed.

"How lovely!" Harold's wife said. "What a beautiful day we've had. The most beautiful day of the year."

"Thanks for the ride," Bobby said as we docked in the marina.

"Thanks for being so enchanting," Harold's wife said.

We bailed out the dinghy from the dock before rowing back to the beach in front of Bobby's house. We were still wringing wet as we dragged the dinghy ashore. But somehow it didn't occur to us until Nita met us at the door.

"What a couple of wet rats you are!" she gasped.

"We're enchanting!" Bobby crooned, giving his mother a wet kiss.

"Well, I'm going to enchant you if you dare step in my house," she warned, bringing us an ocean of towels and clothes.

I changed quickly in the bathroom off the kitchen. I was dripping and shivering and trying not to do either. I loved Nita Muscovi. There wasn't anything in the world I wouldn't do for her. She wasn't like any other mother. She had golden hair that went down to her waist and a face that was so perfect and beautiful, and sometimes sad, that you couldn't, and didn't want to, ever stop looking at it.

She always smelled fresh, like soap, and the things inside her house always smelled of lemon scent or something baking with cinnamon in it or just the sea breeze blowing through her white starched curtains.

Teeny was sitting at the kitchen table in front of a mixing bowl. Her face and hands were covered with chocolate frosting. The uniced cake waited on the countertop.

"Teeny!" Nita moaned.

"I just ate a little," Teeny said plaintively, holding up her hands to be wiped.

"You've made a mess of it, little girl."

Nita tried to be mad, but couldn't. Laughing, she stood Teeny up on the kitchen stool and sponged her off.

"Did Bobby and Eve go swimming?" she asked Nita.

"No, they were shipwrecked."

"What's 'shipwreck'?" Teeny wanted to know.

"Like the party we're having for Bobby and Eve's class. Their boat has been run aground in a storm—that's being shipwrecked. And they're on a tropical island with nothing but coconuts to eat!"

"Coconuts!" Teeny exclaimed.

21

"You're coconuts," Bobby teased.

"You're coconuts!"

"Teeny, you don't have to scream," Nita said in a quiet but firm voice. "Eve, I was wondering if your mother would be a chaperone."

It was as if a light had flooded the room. "Oh, yes, yes. I'm sure she would. She never gets asked to do anything since people think she'd be too busy. And she kind of is. But I know she would. I'll go ask her now."

Nita laughed. "It's not that urgent. Can't you stay for lunch first?"

I wished so much Mum could be a class mother like Nita. It was the last year I'd ever have class mothers. Class mothers planned all our parties and chaperoned us on field trips. At the end of the year, we made presents for them and sang songs to them at a special P.T.A. meeting in their honor. I wished so much Mum could be honored like that.

After lunch, I hurried back up the hill. Mum was upstairs putting away lunch dishes. I bounced in and slammed the door behind me.

"Evie!" Mum said with a jump. "Your father's sleeping."

"Mum, guess what! Nita wants to know if you can be a chaperone for our shipwreck party. Please say yes, Mum. It'll be so much fun." I threw my arms around her neck and hung down like a sack of potatoes.

"Evie, let go."

"Please, Mum, please!"

"All right, all right. You're breaking my neck. When is it?"

"In two weeks. Oh, Mum, we'll have so much fun. Our first big party. You've never come to any of my parties."

"I said I'd come now, didn't I? Now hush, you'll wake your father. I have to go back downstairs."

I trailed eagerly after her. "Mum, can I have some ice cream?"

"Ice cream? Didn't you eat lunch at Bobby's?"

"Yes. But I want some ice cream. Nita's taking Bobby to get

22

new sneakers this afternoon and asked if I could go along. Can I, Mum?"

"Evie, you spend all your time over there. You're going to wear Nita out."

"No, I won't, Mum."

"And I wish you'd stop calling her 'Nita.' It isn't polite."

"But she wants me to call her Nita."

Chantel made a face as we walked into the store. "I'm going over to Janet's for lunch," she informed Mum crossly.

"Well, don't be gone long," Mum said.

"You won't see her the rest of the afternoon," I said to Mum as Chantel rushed out.

Mum sighed. "What am I going to do with her?"

"Let her baby-sit. I'll help you out, Mum."

"She has to show she's responsible here first."

I pulled an ice cream bar out of the freezer and sat down on one of the stools. "I'll stay here, Mum," I said with a twinge of conscience. "I don't have to go with Nita and Bobby."

"No, you go ahead. I can manage."

"No, I'll stay, Mum. You can teach me the cash register." It was the one thing she wouldn't let me touch in the store, the one thing above all else I wanted to learn. Like the Morse, it had its own special code that made the bell ring and the cash drawer magically fly open. There was a compartment for each number of bill and each kind of coin. Mum would bring rolls of shiny new coins from the bank and spill them into each drawer like water. It seemed a monumental amount of money to me.

I began swiveling in circles on the stool, licking my ice cream and looking up at the ceiling to see if I could keep from falling off.

"Bobby got a letter from his dad today," I went on, not wanting to sound *too* eager about the cash register.

"Oh, really?" Mum said brightly. "What did it say?"

"His dad is a hero already. He rescued all these wounded men in a rice paddy. Bobby says he'll get a hundred Silver Stars for it."

23

"Well, now."

"Mum, did Daddy ever get a Silver Star when he was in the war?"

Mum started a new pot of coffee gurgling. "No, I don't believe he saw that kind of action, Evie," she said distractedly.

"Well, what did he do that was brave?"

"You'll have to ask him."

"But he doesn't remember anything. Or doesn't want to."

"He asked me to marry him. I suppose that was brave."

I began spinning faster. "Why was that brave?"

"Oh, enough questions for now," Mum said, suddenly impatient. "Someday when a young man asks you to marry him, you'll understand."

"Did you feel weird when you got engaged to Daddy?"

"Barbara Eve, get off that stool — you're making me dizzy. There's nothing weird about getting engaged. It's exciting. Now, get off that stool."

I took a flying leap and landed against the door, jangling the bells and dripping ice cream all down my freshly laundered t-shirt.

"Evie," Mum said, frowning. "If you're going to goof off, you might as well go with Bobby."

"No, Mum, I'll go call him and tell him I can't. And can I learn the cash register? Please?"

She sighed and looked at me, still frowning. It was her exasperated, "I-give-up" look. "All right, yes."

I raced back upstairs, two at a time, too afraid she'd change her mind about the party *and* the cash register to say another word.

I put the ice cream in the freezer and quickly sponged off my shirt at the sink. I caught my reflection in the toaster and, bending close to it, pursed up my lips and closed my eyes to slits the way movie stars did when they wanted to kiss. My reflection was as obtuse as a puckering mackerel.

Giggling, I picked up the phone. What if that was the way it looked really? But I knew I didn't have any "ideas," not the way Daddy said it. If they were the same kind of "ideas" Chantel liked to talk about. Today there was the Cove, and the water, alive and sparkling and gripping cold, silver-coated mackerel, white sailboats, as white as any cloud, and Morse Codes and shipwreck parties and cash register bells, all on the most beautiful day of the year. Those were my ideas.

2

"THERE," Chantel said, fastening a giant plastic purple orchid in my hair. "You look gorgeous."

I looked uncertainly in the mirror at my ripped t-shirt and Mum's old gardening pants, rolled up to my knees and bunched around my waist with packing twine. They were lime green with dirt stains all down the front.

"You look like a wreck all right," Chantel giggled, falling back on her bed. "I wish I was going to a shipwreck party. How romantic! Only I couldn't decide who I'd want to be shipwrecked with. Too many to choose from."

She sprawled on her stomach across her bed and began flipping through a glamour magazine. Her dark hair rippled down her back and across the flushed sides of her face while her feet stuck straight up behind her, twitching back and forth in two ruffled pink slippers. The rest of her was in bra and panties and that was it.

"It must be boring to have just *one* boyfriend," she sighed.

"That's all you ever think about." The orchid was looking more and more like someone had tied a purple balloon onto my head.

"Well, let me tell you something. It's the *only* thing, believe me."

"It is not. Unless you have jelly for a brain, which apparently you do."

I headed for the door when Chantel suddenly let out a squawk. She jumped off her bed and grabbing me, twirled me around in front of the mirror. "Your *undershirt* shows right through your t-shirt! I just noticed. Gad, why doesn't Mum get you a bra?"

Horrified, I stared into the mirror and saw she was right. You could see the little pink roses and bows right through the thin cotton of my t-shirt.

I yanked the orchid out of my hair and threw it at her. "I hate you," I said, feeling sudden, angry tears. "Why do I have to live with you in the same room? I can never get away from you. I wish you'd just shut up and leave me alone!"

I rushed furiously into the bathroom and locked the door. Still trembling, I banged the toilet lid down and plunked down on top of it. It was an ugly bathroom, all cracked, pink tile with raggedy yellow and green towels that didn't match and a plastic orange-turned-brown shower curtain with bloated green fish swimming on it. There was a yellow rug next to the tub with a big green daisy stuck in the middle of it, and it was covered with little white and blue pieces of lint and long, curling strands of Chantel's hair. Chantel's hair was all over the bathroom. It was plastered to the sides of the sink and the drain in the tub and over the back of the toilet. It drove Mum nuts.

Chantel's bras and fish-net stockings were all over the bathroom, too. She washed them out every night. I sat there on the cold lid and stared fiercely at the three lace bras, two white and one pink, delicately drip-drying from a hosiery hanger over the shower nozzle. They were absurdly grotesque-looking things, padded an inch thick with foam. Why Chantel wanted to look any more bosomy than she already was was beyond me. She had a girdle up there, too, with little clips on it to hook her fish-nets to, and I couldn't understand why she wanted to strap herself into that contraption any more than those bras. Foam rubber armor was what it all looked like to me.

Because I knew it would make her mad, I jumped up and pulled the pink one off the hanger. It was still damp and smelled like rose-scented soap. I inspected the foam padding for a few seconds and then carefully slipped one arm through a limp, pink strap, then the other. Then I had a better idea. I pulled it off, then my shirt. I put the bra back on over my rose-festooned under-

27

shirt. I couldn't make it hook in the back, so I tied the sides in a big knot and pulled my t-shirt back on. For three minutes I stood in front of the mirror and stared.

Suddenly, Mum was pounding on the door. "Evie, are you ready? It's time to go."

Feeling a wave of revulsion, I whipped the shirt over my head and began struggling with Chantel's knotted bra. Finally, I just slipped it over my head, too, and flung it against the bathtub wall.

"Barbara Eve, what are you doing in there? Let's go!"

"I'm not going!" I announced firmly. Yanking down the rest of Chantel's armor, I then heaved up the window sash and tossed them all down into the McElheny's backyard. The bras floated into the flower bed, but the girdle made a glorious landing on top of the doghouse.

There was a long silence from the other side of the door, then a shocked, "Why not?" The door knob began to rattle.

I was trying hard not to giggle. "Because—I'm—not—going!"

"Evie, open this door! What do you mean you're not going? How's it going to look if I show up at your party and you don't?"

I riveted myself to the toilet seat again and helplessly folded my arms against my flat, loathsome undershirt. "I'm not going and I don't care!"

"Barbara Eve Cooper, open the door this minute, do you hear me?" Mum's voice was beginning to rattle like the door knob. Then I heard her turn and march down the hall to our bedroom. As if she were at the end of a long tunnel, I heard a distant, "Chantel, what did you say to her? Honestly, your sister's first big party. Can't you show her any respect?"

Chantel was whining back something, and as I sat there, I began to think of all the things she had spoiled, including my one and only birthday party when she had sulked the whole time because of the dress Mum made her wear and how afterward she made fun of all my presents.

"I hate her! I hate her! I hate her!" I chanted, kicking at the base of the toilet.

Mum's voice came back, gently this time. "Evie, would you please open the door so I can talk to you?"

I didn't say anything, but kept ramming my heels against the veined porcelain. I started whistling.

"Evie, sweetheart, please let me talk to you. I won't be cross."

Sighing, I shuffled to the door and poised my hand over the knob a few seconds before slowly turning it. Mum nudged the door open and peeked in.

"Evie, what happened?" She poked her head through, took one look at my t-shirt on the rug and me in my undershirt, and somehow the idea quickly sunk in.

Closing the door behind her, she looked at me with the same faint smile she always used to cover up her real feelings.

"What did she say to you, Evie?"

Since it was the only place to sit, I sat back down on the cold toilet seat. I took a deep breath, fighting back tears. "I'm so sick and tired of Chantel picking on me. She said you could see my undershirt through my t-shirt."

Mum sighed, picked up the t-shirt, and held it out in front of her, trying to see through it. Her eyes seemed misty, gray rather than blue, and she put out her dry, red hand to touch my hair. Mum's skin was bad. It was always cracking and bleeding. But I loved her hands more than anyone else's in the world.

"Barbara Eve, no one but Chantel would notice what she did, don't you know that?"

"I hate Chantel," I sobbed. "I hate her and I hate myself. She always has to spoil everything."

Mum sat down on the edge of the tub and pulled me onto her lap. I couldn't stop crying now, and the more Mum held me and stroked my flat hair, the harder I cried.

"You're my baby, Barbara Eve. Don't ever forget, you're my baby and I love you. You've been looking forward to this party so much and had such fun helping Nita and Bobby decorate. You're going to the party, and you're going to have a wonderful time, and nothing is going to spoil it for you unless you spoil it yourself."

I knew Mum was right. I thought of all the fun I'd had shopping with Nita and Bobby, of the leis we'd made out of Kleenex, and the funny records we'd found at the library. Nita had even made us hot dogs while we watched the World Series and strung the leis together. The invincible Red Sox blew it in the final game. The St. Louis Cardinals won the Series, and Bobby had become terribly gloomy.

"I'm sick of wearing these stupid undershirts. I feel like a baby."

"Well, maybe you're right," Mum said thoughtfully. "We'll go shopping soon."

"I'm not wearing any stupid bra like Chantel," I said emphatically. Horses couldn't drag me into wearing one.

"Not like Chantel's. One your size."

There was a timid knock on the door; then Chantel peeked in. She looked quizzically at me for a moment, then at Mum, then lowered her eyes. "Evie, I didn't mean to make fun of you. I'm sorry. I hope you have a good time at the party."

She stood there in the door, awkwardly clutching her robe. I knew Mum had made her come apologize.

"Thanks, Chantel," I said quietly, trying to suppress a smile.

I wondered how long it would take her to notice her underwear was missing.

Mum quickly rigged me up in an old sweatshirt with holes in it that didn't show anything. Then we marched down the hill, hiding our costumes under our raincoats. Mum was wearing an old skirt with the hem dragging out of it, and it showed behind her coat like a tail.

"Imagine if anyone saw us," Mum whispered with a girlish giggle. "We look like a pair of ragamuffins."

There was already a pile of cars parked in front of Bobby's house. I began to feel excited again. I looked admiringly at Mum, and she smiled as I rang the doorbell.

Bobby opened the door with a "There you are!" He was wearing his bleached-out cutoffs and a fake beard that hung down to his stomach.

"Where'd you get that?" I shrieked.

"I grew it. What are you wearing raincoats for? Hello, Mrs. Cooper."

"Hello. Robinson Crusoe, I presume?"

"Uh, yes, Madame," Bobby said, imitating Mum's accent and bowing over his beard.

Mum politely bowed back. Then we stepped inside. It was no longer Nita's casual living room but a tropical rain forest. There were palm trees made out of cardboard and green plastic and twining crepe paper vines, and a waterfall made out of real rocks and shimmering silver streamers. Teeny's stuffed monkey swung from one of the trees. Giant paper flowers bloomed everywhere, and in the background, a record was playing the sounds of a tropical rainstorm, thumping drums, and birdcalls.

Nita came out, not looking like Nita at all. She was wearing a checkered shift with patches sewn all over it and a dog bone tied over her ponytail.

"Hi!" she said brightly. "Come on in and take your coats off, for pete's sake. This is a tropical island!"

"Well, we were a bit embarrassed to be seen walking down the street looking like a couple of tramps," Mum said, handing over her raincoat.

I took mine off, too, although still somewhat reluctantly. I didn't think I looked either really funny or really pretty in a costume. Just a little lost and a little weird.

"The other mothers are here," Nita said. "Everyone's outside making the punch."

On the patio were more palm trees and tables set with leis and seashells. The mothers were gathered around a large scrub tub, pouring in bottles of juice and ginger ale. No one was dressed for a shipwreck party, except Dana Moore's mother who looked like a giant rosebush in a green and red flowered muumuu.

"I'm so glad you dressed up," Nita whispered to Mum. "Nobody else did."

The kids were down on the beach playing tag. Except for Dana Moore who suddenly came out of the kitchen with a tray of celery sticks filled with cream cheese. She was wearing a miniature version of her mother's muumuu.

"Hello, Eve," she said, standing close to Bobby. "Doesn't Bobby look crazy? And where'd you get those pants? You look pretty crazy yourself."

"Thanks."

Suddenly, I could hear Nita's convulsive laughter. Then Mr. Hughes, unmistakably Mr. Hughes, dressed like a beach bum, walked outside. He was in rags from head to foot, and even his toes were sticking out of a pair of battered boots. I stared at him in disbelief.

"Mr. Hughes!" Dana screeched. "You are *crazy*!"

"I caught the boots fishing today," he said, his eyes shining brightly. The late summer sun was still burned hot pink in his fair face and towards the top of his balding head where his hat was pushed back. There was nothing nervous or silly about him, just an excitement, and I suddenly began to laugh.

The mothers came out to fuss over him, and Bobby slid back inside. Dana glided off to arrange her celery sticks. I turned to watch the kids on the beach, but they had disappeared. Softly, a small hand slipped into mine. It was Teeny in her grass skirt.

"Hi, Eve," she said with a forlorn look on her face. "You want to see my shells?"

"Sure, Teeny."

She was feeling left out. I'd already seen her shells a hundred times, but I let her lead me around the tables.

"See, I put them on the tables for Mommy," she said proudly.

I squeezed her hand. "You did a good job, Teeny."

More kids were arriving. It was almost time to eat. We gathered hungrily around the large kettles outside, steaming with layers of fish, potatoes, and corn on the boil.

"Eve, why don't you go round up the kids on the beach?" Nita asked.

"Sure!" I responded enthusiastically. I ran towards the wall, then stopped. The beach looked still and empty.

Puzzled, I ran down the steps and across the sand, waving my arms. Before I could yell, there was a sudden whoop. Ronny Engels, dressed like a pirate with a black patch over one eye, came galloping out from behind the rocks. The others charged closely after him as if racing to be the first ones back.

"It's a baby whale!" Ronny screamed up at everyone. "It's washed ashore!"

"A whale? Oh yeah? Where?" Mr. Hughes called down.

"Behind the rocks. Come see. We just found it."

"You're lying," I challenged him.

"You're a scaredy-cat," he fired back.

By now, the commotion was so loud and so urgent that everyone was curious to see what exactly they had found. The mothers quickly covered the food, and hurried after the kids. Mr. Hughes kicked off his raggedy boots and ran, too, like a big feathered bird, his tattered clothes flying behind him.

There had never been a beached whale on our island, not that anybody ever knew about. We'd heard about them beaching farther north or along the Cape, but never in Musk Cove.

Still disbelieving, I walked instead of running, my heart beating loudly nonetheless. Then we all saw it, a small, black rubbery creature awash with seaweed. It was perfectly round and still except for a fin sticking strangely in the air.

Everyone came to an abrupt halt, and for a split second, there was an awful, wonderful silence as if something both dreadful and important had been discovered.

"That's not a whale!" someone exclaimed sharply.

Bobby moved forward with Dana hanging onto him and gave it a kick. Then he pulled off the "fin" and held it up. The creature was nothing more than a mound of sand covered with pieces of black tarpaulin and seaweed.

"Engels, you faker!" he yelled.

Howling with laughter, Ronny had to double over and clutch his stomach. Bobby jerked free from Dana and grabbing Ronny around the waist, knocked him over into the water.

"Boys! Boys!" the mothers yelled.

But no one paid any attention. Ronny pulled Bobby down into the water with him, and after that everybody wanted in on it. Feeling exhilarated by it all, I waded into the water as well. Ronny turned and pushed me seat down so that my green pantaloons ballooned out over the incoming wave like a jellyfish. At that instant, I saw Dana standing back, watching and cringing. I scooped up a handful of wet sand and heaved it at her. She didn't seem to know where it came from and burst out crying.

Since no one paid any attention to the mothers, Mr. Hughes splashed in and grabbed Bobby and Ronny by the backs of their shirts. Everyone in the water stood up straight then, shivering and hanging his head. That's when I realized I was the only girl out there.

"Cool it! What's gotten into you two?" Mr. Hughes barked.

"It was a stupid joke!" Bobby's beard had fallen off. He was breathing angrily, angrier than I'd ever seen him.

"I'm bleeding," Ronny whined, dabbing his fingers at his lip. "Gosh, it was just a joke."

"Ronny, I think you owe everyone here an apology," his mother said, swiping at him with a handkerchief.

Ronny tried to pull away from her. "I'm sorry."

"I don't think we'll stay," Mrs. Engels said to Nita. "I'm awfully sorry Ronny spoiled the party."

"No, please don't go," Nita pleaded. "He hasn't spoiled the party." She was standing behind Bobby with her arms around him, and her face was anxious and sad.

"I think he's caused enough trouble for one evening," snapped Mrs. Engels. "He knows he shouldn't provoke Bobby. After all . . ."

"Bobby's the host. He shouldn't have provoked Ronny," Nita went on in her calm voice.

Bobby took a deep breath and sighed. "Look, Ronny, I'm sorry I got mad. I'm sorry I hit you."

"Yeah, well, it's okay," Ronny said.

They slapped their palms together and headed up the beach. It was embarrassing to have to apologize in front of your mother, teacher, and everybody else. I darted a glance at Mum who was frowning suspiciously at me.

"I don't know who threw that wet sand all over Dana, but it was very cruel," I could hear Mrs. Moore complaining. "I guess

these children just aren't mature enough yet to handle them-
selves at a mixed party."

She stormed off with Dana while the other mothers gathered
the rest of the kids and herded them back up the beach. Mum
had Teeny, and I hung in back of her, wanting to hear what Nita
was saying to Mr. Hughes.

"He never used to have a temper. Now the slightest thing
sets him off. I'm afraid it's getting worse. When the Sox lost the
Series, he was terribly upset. He's afraid, I think, his father won't
come home."

"It's hard when a boy loses his father, even temporarily. All
of you are dealing with that now."

"Well, that's why I'm so glad he has you for a teacher this
year. He already raves about you. You'll be good for him."

I looked back over my shoulder. They were walking side by
side, now in the shadows, looking like some primitive couple just
risen from the sea. She looked at me and smiled, her face
confident and happy again.

3

MR. HUGHES asked us to write down our ideas for our science projects. We were supposed to pick subjects that would hold our interest for the entire year since we'd do three reports about them. A Report: Cover the history of your subject. B Report: What uses or functions does your subject serve today? C Report: Present your subject to the class in a creative way, such as an experiment, a poem or story, a shadow box, or art work.

I wrote glumly to Mr. Hughes:

It was my idea to do my project on whales because they seem interesting to me and I'd like to know more about them especially since they live in the ocean and perhaps swim by every day and we don't even know it. But now everyone would think it was a joke and I can't decide what else to do except maybe sharks.

Mr. Hughes wrote back on my paper:

I think a project on whales would be fine, and don't let practical jokes get you down, and cut out the run-on sentences.

Bobby wanted to do his project on bombs, but Nita didn't think he should be concentrating on bombs all year long, so he decided instead on electricity. Mr. Hughes wrote back on his paper: "Bright idea!"

Miss Higby was the librarian on our island. She wasn't any

taller than us sixth-graders and seemed to shrink even further as we gathered around her at the card catalog. Most of us looked down on her black bun that coiled around the top of her head like a snake. Some of the boys were making antennas out of paper clips and sticking them in it.

A buzz of stifled laughter began circulating around the room. Mr. Hughes suddenly noticed why and had to turn his head aside for a moment.

"Okay, quiet down," he finally ordered, his face beet red from trying not to smile. "Ronny and Curt, come stand by me."

Miss Higby looked up for a moment and blinked. Then confidently she pursued her search through the index cards.

We were supposed to be learning how to research our projects. But at the moment the library itself seemed of more interest to me. It was a small castlelike building made of stone, with a vaulted ceiling and a cavernous fireplace in the main reference room. I asked Miss Higby if somebody had lived in the library once since it had such a huge fireplace. She blinked at me as if I'd asked a dumb question.

"No," she said seriously, "when the library was originally built, the fireplace was its only source of heat."

"Why don't they use it anymore then?"

"Well, there are more efficient ways of heating now."

"Oh." It wasn't a very satisfying answer. It took all the mystery out of the place, except for the long glass cases lining the wall filled with Indian relics that had been found on the island. Arrowheads and fragments of pottery hinted at a civilization on the island prior to our own. Some time ago an Indian boy and girl had paddled around Musk Cove. It was interesting to think about.

Mr. Hughes planned for us to be at the library half the afternoon so we could get a good start on our projects. I could only find a few books on whales and mostly the same information in all the encyclopedias. I didn't feel like asking Miss Higby for any ideas.

"Why the frown on your face, Eve?" Mr. Hughes asked.

"I can't find much on whales," I replied grimly.

"You may have to do more digging and write for information. We've discussed ways of doing that."

I sighed. "I guess you're right."

Mr. Hughes winked. "Don't get discouraged now. There are many sources of information you can tap into."

I didn't want to tap into anything at the moment. I stared at the yellow, green, and black version of the American flag in the encyclopedia under "Optical Illusion." After staring at it for thirty seconds, if you looked at a blank piece of paper, you'd see the flag in its true red, white, and blue colors.

"The whale is a mysterious creature," I wrote through the red and white bars of the American flag on my notebook paper. "It is the largest mammal in the world known to man. But nobody seems to know much about them. At least, not too much has been written about them. Mostly, they are for killing, it seems."

That was depressing. I fidgeted and found some more places to write to about whales. Then it was time to go. Miss Higby finally smiled and thanked us for coming, but it was more like thanking us for leaving. As we left, the antennas were hanging a little lopsided out of her bun.

The air was smacking-crisp outside. The island was alive with fall color. Orange, red, and yellow leaves fluttered past us on our walk back to school. Soon I would be able to see the Cove sparkling through them.

Bobby broke through my reverie and offered me his apple left over from lunch.

"Did you find anything for your project?" he asked.

"No, there's not much on whales. Maybe I should have picked something else."

"You picked right. You'll find stuff. There's almost *too* much to read about electricity."

I crunched into the apple, catching the tart juice with my tongue. It was a perfect apple.

"I have to go to the dentist today," Bobby said as we walked into the school yard. "So I can't walk home with you."

Nita was waiting for him in the car with Teeny. She waved happily at us and Mr. Hughes who strolled over to greet her.

"Hi," he said. "Hi, Teeny. How are you?"

"Oh, we're just fine, Mr. Hughes," Nita answered breezily. "That may change though. We're going to the dentist."

"Sounds like an exciting afternoon."

"Listen, can you come for dinner next Friday if you haven't any plans? Bobby and I have been discussing how much we'd like to have you over, and I understand it's your birthday!"

Mr. Hughes turned a rosy pink. "How'd you know? I'd love that. I have no plans, and it'll be a special treat."

"Well, consider this a birthday celebration then. And Evie, you come, too. We'll have a special birthday dinner party."

Bobby winked at me and slid into the backseat. I laughed, unable to say anything. Mr. Hughes's birthday celebration? I couldn't imagine anything more fun.

"We'll see you next Friday at six, then?"

"I'll be there."

All day Friday the class squirmed and wiggled, passing notes and stifling giggles until the suspense was more than we could bear.

"All right, I've about had it with this class today," Mr. Hughes said gruffly, snapping his history book shut. "Get out a piece of paper and write a composition on one of the explorers we've been talking about, what he discovered, and the hardships he overcame."

There were a few moans, but not the usual. We knew it wouldn't last much longer.

"I want these handed in at the bell, and they'll be graded." Mr. Hughes sat down at his desk and rubbed his temples for a moment. It was a bad thing to frustrate your favorite teacher on his birthday. But it couldn't be helped. I doodled for a while, then nervously began writing in case he really was mad and stayed serious about collecting our compositions.

The class grew eerily quiet. Mr. Hughes looked up at us, watching intently. Then, still watching us, he wadded up a sheet of paper and tossed it towards the waste can a few feet from his desk. It missed.

It was too much. We leaned out of our seats, squeaking and batting back the tears, afraid of exploding our insides any minute.

"Get back to work!" Mr. Hughes ordered, picking up the wad and dunking it in this time. He didn't smile, either.

Then the back door suddenly opened, and there stood Nita and Teeny and all the other room mothers with a big white cake full of glowing candles.

"SURPRISE!" we screamed, at last rescuing our party blowers from the depths of our desks and giving them full attention.

Mr. Hughes dropped his face into his hands, then came back up again, smiling and red as a lobster.

Shaking his head, he laughed as the mothers started us on a rousing chorus of "Happy Birthday."

"Do we still have to turn in our compositions?" one boy yelled.

"Save them for tomorrow." But we all knew he'd changed his mind. "How many candles have you got on there?" Mr. Hughes asked.

"Lots!" Nita said, laughing.

"Give me a count," he told us, taking in his breath.

"*One . . . two . . . three!*" we all shouted. He blew them all out in one blow, except three, and then it took him two blows to get those out. His face was redder than anyone had ever seen it, like a big red balloon ready to burst.

"Thank you all so much," he said, pulling out his hanky and dabbing at his eyes. They were actually wet.

Nita knew how to do everything right and how to make everybody feel special. It was a large part of what I found so wonderful in her. As much as I loved Mum, I wished Bobby's home was my home, that Mum was Nita, and that I felt and smelled good things when I walked through the door.

That evening, I met Mr. Hughes at the top of the hill. He didn't live on the island, but drove in from the mainland every day to school. I climbed in his car and rode down the hill with him. He was in a gray suit and had a gray felt hat tipped back over his head, like a gangster out of an old movie.

His car was a tank, too, older than any car I'd ever seen except in the movies. I looked at him and giggled.

"What's so funny?" he demanded.

"How old is this car?"

"Probably as old as you."

"I was born in 1956."

"Then it's one year older."

At that point, the car began to spit and rattle and clunk, and we *clunk-clunked* all the way into Bobby's driveway.

"Mr. Hughes, this car is *too* old!"

"Well," he agreed, laughing, "I guess I'm just kind of attached to it."

Nita and Bobby and Teeny came running out.

"Is that your car?" Nita asked.

"I told you he had this real old car," Bobby said admiringly.

"Can we ride in it?" Teeny asked.

"Teeny!"

"Sure you can," Mr. Hughes said, crouching down to Teeny's level. "How about after dinner?"

"Won't that be fun?" Nita said, leading us all into the house. "I've got halibut steaks on the grill. I hope you like halibut, Mr. Hughes."

"Love it. Seafood's my favorite."

"Well, this is as fresh as I could find it. Not from Julio's, mind you."

"I know a joke," Bobby said. "Why did a guy eat a shark whole?"

"Why?" asked Mr. Hughes.

"Just for the halibut. Get it?"

"Oh, Bobby," Nita reprimanded mildly. "Mr. Hughes is your teacher."

"Don't worry, I'm not offended," Mr. Hughes said, smiling.

"Well, I would think there are a lot more appropriate jokes than that one."

"I know a joke," giggled Teeny. "What's black and white and red all over?"

Bobby rolled his eyes. "Uh, oh, here we go."

"I haven't the foggiest idea," Mr. Hughes said, winking at us.

"An embarrassed zebra!" proclaimed Teeny. "Know what else is black and white and red all over?"

"What?"

"A skunk with measles!"

"Teeny has a new joke book," Nita explained.

"I can read, Mr. Hughes," Teeny said proudly. "Want to see?"

Teeny ran for her joke book and read them all to Mr. Hughes, more reciting them from memory than actually reading them. But Mr. Hughes praised her for it. Then Bobby brought out his scrapbook of his dad's pictures and souvenirs.

"Looks like you take after your dad, Bobby," Mr. Hughes remarked.

"Thanks," Bobby said with a quiet pride.

Then it was time to eat. Nita brought in the fish while Bobby and I ceremoniously lit the tall, white candles. Nita had spread out a lacy white tablecloth with her good china and crystal set on it. Between the candles in their brass holders was a bowl of fresh flowers. It was a beautiful table.

Nita sat at one end, and Mr. Hughes at the other while the three of us clustered around like a small bunch of grapes.

"It's so nice to have a full table, Mr. Hughes," Nita said wistfully after we'd said grace. Her eyes sparkled in the candlelight. "Please tell us about your family. We know so little about you."

"There's not much to tell," Mr. Hughes said, helping himself generously from the steaming dishes being passed around. "I was an only child, so there was just my father, mother, and me. Now there's just my mother and me."

"You've lost your father then? I'm so sorry," Nita sympathized.

"Yes, when I was, uh, very young," Mr. Hughes said with hesitation. "He was a wonderful man."

"A lot like you, I'm sure."

"Don't you have any children?" Teeny asked.

Mr. Hughes laughed. "I have lots of children. I get to teach them every day."

"But don't you have any of your very own?"

"No, Teeny, I don't. That's why I became a teacher."

Teeny struggled with this for a few moments, then blurted, "You can come be our daddy. We don't have one anymore."

Nita took a deep breath. "Why, Teeny, yes you do! You know where he is and that he's coming home to us soon."

But Mr. Hughes seemed to know what she meant. He leaned over and winked at her. "I think you want me to be your friend, Teeny. Well, I'd like that."

There were suddenly tears in Nita's eyes. Mr. Hughes winked at her. I winked at Mr. Hughes, and he winked back. Then Bobby and I began winking at each other across the table and at Mr. Hughes and Nita, distorting our faces more and more absurdly with each wink until we made Nita laugh again.

Nobody could wink like Mr. Hughes. He had a way of scrunching up his face and nodding when he did it that made you feel as if he'd told you a little secret. He could wiggle his ears, too. He'd never done that in class before. It was a revelation.

Nita served individual lemon souffles for dessert with a special lemon-blueberry sauce. Bobby and I ate ours hungrily, but Mr. Hughes seemed content to merely sit and admire his.

"All of this, the food, the table, the candles and flowers — it's been the loveliest evening of my life, and the happiest birthday. Thank you."

Nita looked up and smiled warmly, not saying anything. I had never seen her more pleased.

Mr. Hughes insisted on washing dishes after dinner. Nita wrapped him up in her apron and assigned Bobby and me each a dishcloth. Teeny was only allowed to handle the silverware while Nita put the china and crystal away.

"Do you know, 'Row Your Boat'?" Mr. Hughes asked, digging into the suds. "It's the only way to do dishes. Now I'll start, Eve and Bobby come in second, then Nita and Teeny, and we'll have a round. Okay, here we go."

Mr. Hughes had a deep, gusty voice, deeper than we would have imagined. We joined in enthusiastically.

"I sang in a men's chorale for a few years before I began teaching," he said. "'Row Your Boat' was always our final encore."

"You have a wonderful voice," Nita said, happily surprised. "Please sing some more."

"Let's go for a drive and I will."

We clunked and rattled back up the hill and breezed merrily, merrily along the causeway and up the coast. The evening was warm, and we rolled down the windows. Nita took the clips out of her hair and hung her head back. The wind caught her hair and separated it into a hundred snapping gold ribbons.

We hung over the backseat, Bobby, Teeny, and I, listening to Mr. Hughes's rich voice sailing over the wind. He took us all the way to Marblehead where we spilled eagerly out onto the beach.

The sky had sunk into a velvety indigo, dotted here and there with burning stars like diamond chips. It was Indian summer, the last of the warmth before winter. Mr. Hughes's voice began to match the sky. We huddled in the sand, watching and listening.

"You know," he said, suddenly quiet, "there's a school in the Berkshires that keeps asking me to come teach music. What—"

"You can't leave, Mr. Hughes!" we all chorused.

He laughed and threw up his hands. "I'm staying, I'm staying!"

Nita sighed, then shivered. The air had suddenly become cool. "How very beautiful," she murmured, looking up. "Mr. Hughes, what do you think of singing when you see a sky like that?"

There was quiet, a happy, peaceful quiet that says everything is good, even if not perfect. I pretended this evening we really were a family. Then, without pretending, the good feeling told me in a way we were.

Mr. Hughes began to sing, and because we knew the song, we joined in.

Tell me why the stars do shine,
Tell me why the ivy twines,
Tell me why the sky's so blue,
And I will tell you why I love you.
Because God made the stars to shine,
Because God made the ivy twine,
Because God made the sky so blue,
That is the reason why I love you.

4

I was a cold November morning. The last of the autumn leaves lay in damp clumps along the roadsides while a token few continued to hang stubbornly from naked branches against the bristling wind. A fog had settled into the island as thick as Mum's oatmeal. I played around with the latter in my bowl, not wanting to go to school.

"Hurry up, Evie," Mum urged. "Why are you being such a slowpoke?"

"I don't feel good."

Mum looked at me suspiciously. "What's wrong?"

"I don't know. I just don't feel good."

"Where don't you feel good?"

"All over."

Impatiently, I pushed the oatmeal away. Mum came over and put her warm, dry hand against my forehead.

"You don't have a fever. It's just the day, don't you think? Rather ugly out, I'm afraid."

She went to the window and peeked through the curtains.

"I feel *yucky*, Mum," I moaned, dragging myself from the table. I couldn't say what it was exactly, a feeling, a sudden dread of the day.

"Evie, there's a funny light flashing down at the Cove," Mum said with a start in her voice.

"Bobby," I said, rushing to the window with a sudden burst of energy.

"Bobby?" Mum exclaimed. "What's he doing?"

"It's our secret code," I replied reluctantly, grabbing a pencil and piece of paper from my book bag. "It must be important."

"Secret code?" Mum said in disbelief. "You mean like, oh, what's it called?"

"The Morse Code," I told her, hurriedly jotting down the signals.

Mum gazed out the window; then she watched me dotting and dashing across my paper. "Well, isn't this clever!"

I ran into the bedroom where Chantel was lazily pulling on her stockings. Before she could ask any questions, I pulled my flashlight out of a drawer and hurried into the living room. At the large window, I flashed back that I'd received his message.

"What does he want?" Mum asked.

"Meet . . . me . . . at . . . the . . . Cove," I slowly translated.

"I gotta go, Mum," I said, kissing her cheek.

"Evie . . ."

I didn't look at her, but grabbed my coat and book bag and fled down the stairs.

"Evie," Mum called after me. But I was already halfway down the hill.

In the lonely distance, a foghorn wailed low and deep. Boston Light made a small, piercing spark in response. Bobby was staring out at it from the stone wall.

He looked almost faceless in his blue woolen cap and high-collared jacket. When he saw me, he turned away.

"Bobby, what happened?" I demanded, climbing up on the wall next to him.

He was holding the flashlight in his hands. "My dad," he said softly.

"Is he hurt?"

"He's dead." He stopped for a moment as if afraid of crying. "His helicopter was shot down. We found out last night."

Silently, I put my arm around him, not knowing what to say or how to keep my own tears from falling.

"I have to go take care of my mom," he said, suddenly stiffening. "Mr. Hughes knows I won't be in school for a few days. But I wanted to tell you."

Then, abruptly, he stood up on the wall, facing the beach. "Why'd he have to die? He was my dad." His voice was sobbing now. Before I could touch him, he jumped down onto the sand, stumbled, and then ran towards home.

"Bobby!"

He didn't stop, but kept running until he disappeared into the outstretched fog.

I stood alone on the wall, watching for a few moments. The Cove had become a dim, ghostly blur. In back of me, the houses seemed in motion, floating like shadows in a dream. Suddenly terrified, I raced back up the hill where Mum was waiting at the top of the stairs. She didn't ask a thing, but let me bury my face in her old, fuzzy sweater.

"He's dead, isn't he?" Mum said after a little while. She fished her hanky out of her pocket and let me wipe my face.

"Mum, I prayed every night," I answered her, "but God didn't answer my prayers. He let Bobby's dad be killed. Why?"

"I don't know, love," Mum said gently. "Sometimes God doesn't answer our prayers the way we want Him to."

"Then what's the use of praying if bad things happen instead of good?"

"You can't tell God what to do, Barbara Eve. He won't listen to that kind of prayer."

"Well, I hate God, then."

"Sometimes I've hated Him myself. But that doesn't change anything. Just makes it worse."

I looked up into Mum's face, trying to read what was there. But Mum's face never changed.

"Why have you hated God?" I asked her. "Because of Daddy?"

"Sometimes. But then I get tired of so much hate. It takes all of you to hate as much as it takes all of you to love."

Exhausted from weeping, I hung onto Mum like a trembling leaf. "Mum, it's so bad. Bobby hurts so bad, I can't bear it."

"It hurts you, too, doesn't it?"

"Yes, Mum. Bobby's my best friend. It's not like what Daddy and Chantel say."

"I know, Evie dear. I know."

"Mum, I don't want to go to school."

Mum tried to pry me loose. "Don't you think you'd feel better if you did?"

"No," I pleaded, clinging more desperately.

"I think you will. Mr. Hughes will make you feel better."

I began to cry again. "No, Mum, I don't want to."

Mum firmly took my chin between her thumb and forefinger and lifted my face. "Listen to me now, Barbara Eve. Bobby's daddy is dead, and you've got to think of Bobby now, not yourself. He'll need your help catching up when he comes back. That's what a best friend would do, right?"

I looked into her hazy blue-gray eyes and nodded.

"Now, come on. I'll walk you over to school before Daddy wakes up."

We walked in silence together down the fog-hidden streets towards the school. At the classroom door, Mum kissed me and whispered, "Be brave, Evie." When I turned around, she was gone.

Mr. Hughes was sitting on the edge of his desk. He looked up at me and nodded with understanding. "Hello, Eve. I'm glad you're here."

I quickly sat down, not looking at anyone. The room was quiet. Mr. Hughes flipped a piece of chalk round and round in his fingers, and then hitched up the knees of his pants. A pair of bright blue socks flashed out at everybody.

"We're all hurting for Bobby and his family," he said. His eyes were bright and shiny, and he turned to cough. He kept coughing until finally he pulled a peppermint out of his pocket and popped it into his mouth.

"Perhaps it would be better if we started out asking questions. I wonder if you all are aware of why we're fighting a war in Viet Nam. You tell me what you know or think you know."

I cupped my face in my hands and stared sullenly at my desk. I didn't care about Viet Nam or why there was a war. I hated Viet Nam.

Dana Moore raised her hand. "My father says President Johnson is sending our troops over to Viet Nam to fight the Communists and keep the peace. I think he's doing the right thing, don't you, otherwise someday the Communists may take over the world, and we'd lose our freedom."

"What freedoms would we lose, Dana?" Mr. Hughes asked.

"Oh, the Communists won't let you leave the country or teach religion or own any property. And if you do, they arrest you and throw you in jail or shoot you."

"Why is our freedom important?" Mr. Hughes said, ignoring Dana and looking around the classroom instead.

"Who wants to get shot?" piped a voice in the back.

A few kids snickered. Dana raised her hand again, but Mr. Hughes called on Ronny Engels.

"Our freedom is important because, that way, we can run our own lives and not have somebody else tell us what to do."

Mr. Hughes smiled and flashed his blue socks again. "Is that freedom though? Do your parents let you run your own life?"

Ronny guffawed. "Naw, are you kidding?"

"Maybe we should define freedom first, and then decide why it's important."

Mr. Hughes went to the chalkboard and wrote FREEDOM in large, block letters. He underlined it and, with one hand ready to write, started pointing at waving arms with the other.

"Liberty."

"Choices."

"Happiness."

"No homework!"

"Being free."

"Summer vacation."

"No war."

"Life."

"Peace."

He pointed at me even though I hadn't raised my hand. I was thinking of the times in the dinghy with Bobby, rocking gently in the blue-green waves with the gulls circling overhead. The wind carried them so effortlessly wherever they wanted to go.

I said simply, "Flying. Birds are free."

"A bird is a beautiful symbol of freedom, isn't it? One of our national symbols is the eagle. Thank you, Eve. Can anyone think of another symbolic bird?"

Nobody answered.

"How about the dove? A symbol of peace. John, I believe you mentioned peace, didn't you? I think freedom and peace are meant to go together. Without freedom, there will always be war."

Mr. Hughes turned to look at the chalkboard, contemplating it a moment with his large, bushy eyebrows drawn together over his nose.

"Well," he said, turning back around with a flip of his chalk. "Now we can see why freedom is important, for all people. It gives us the liberty to make choices, and that brings happiness, peace, and life, depending on if the choices are good choices, of course, and if good people are making those choices. I'm going to add something else here."

He scribbled the word, *GROWTH*.

"Let's go back to Eve's example of flying. If a young bird's wings are clipped and never allowed to grow, will that bird learn to fly?"

There was a chorus of muffled "no's!"

Mr. Hughes looked at us intently. "Without the freedom to grow in our minds and our bodies, life will always be stifled. That's why Bobby's father went to war, and why he gave his life. He believed in this country; he believed in you. Let's not ever, *ever* forget that, whether this war is a just war or not, and many people are saying it is not. Men like Bobby's father deserve our deepest respect."

There was a sudden hush in the room, silent enough to hear the click of the minute hand on the large, round wall clock over the door. Mr. Hughes's face had turned bright red and his eyes were glistening. His head was cocked at an angle as if listening to something far away, and his gaze went beyond us, through the starred composition papers on the bulletin board at the back of the room, through the wall of the building, past the playground, and farther still towards something we could not see. No one dared move an inch. We all looked down at our hands.

Mr. Hughes rubbed the corners of his eyes with his fingers, and then got off his desk. "Now," he said forcefully, "who said no homework was freedom?"

There were loud sounds of relief as everyone began twisting, turning, itching, and coughing again.

"Homework's hard, isn't it? You have to make yourself do it sometimes whether you want to or not. Or else your parents make you do it. But you have a choice, don't you? You don't have to do it. And if there wasn't homework at all, you wouldn't have to do it, either. But what would the consequences be? Would you learn? Would you grow? I'm going to add another word to our list."

And in another quick scrawl, he wrote, *RESPONSIBILITY.*

"There have to be some rules and laws, don't you agree? Without them, there wouldn't be freedom, only chaos. Our streets wouldn't be safe to walk on; no one would dare drive a car."

I fidgeted with a rubber eraser and scowled. Suddenly, I felt Mr. Hughes's searching gaze.

"Eve, what do you think?" he said.

"I don't think it matters. Bobby's dad is dead, that's all."

"Perhaps we've left out the most important word," Mr. Hughes said thoughtfully.

Down at the bottom of the board, he wrote, *LOVE.*

I stared at it for awhile, afraid Mr. Hughes was going to ask more questions, but he didn't. He couldn't.

"It hurts to love, sometimes, doesn't it?" he said to me quietly. "But it's the greatest freedom. It's the only thing that truly frees us from ourselves. Bobby will need our love and support when he comes back. I hope all of you will give it to him and not be afraid."

Mr. Hughes and the class talked some more about being afraid, about death, but I didn't want to listen. I cupped my hands over my ears instead and stared down into my history book.

"I thought perhaps we could make a card for Bobby and his family," Mr. Hughes suggested. "I'd like you to draw a picture or write a short poem that we can put into a book for them. Let it reflect your love and friendship for Bobby."

I drew the Cove. I colored the water summer blue-green and the dinghy half-red, half-black, the way it was. I put in the gulls and Bracken's Hill, and then in the distance I whimsically drew a spouting whale. The hurt of the morning eased a little, and I began to wonder if it really was true. Perhaps, after all, it *was* a mistake, and Bobby's dad wasn't dead.

After that, we had geometry instead of arithmetic. I didn't mind geometry the way I did arithmetic. Numbers were an exasperating business. But circles and squares and triangles were things you could have fun with. There was something nice about being able to make a perfect circle with a compass and knowing you could make a point on a piece of paper and somehow connect it with a star. That was the way Mr. Hughes taught us geometry.

Mr. Hughes kept us busy so that the day went quickly. At the last bell, I ran out the door and was halfway down the street towards home when I remembered I'd left my geometry homework in my desk.

Irritated, I turned back. The school yard was empty. I walked down the dark, waxy-smelling hallway alone. The classroom door was slightly ajar, so I reached out to push it open. Through the widening column of light, I could see Mr. Hughes bowed over his desk, his face in his hands. I didn't understand at first. Then the realization that he was crying cemented my feet to the floor. I stood helplessly watching the door swing into the room.

The lights were off in the classroom. Mr. Hughes suddenly lifted his head and looked at me. Startled, he didn't get up, but blew his nose with his hanky.

"I forgot my homework," I said numbly, still unable to move from the doorway.

"Well," he said, stuffing his hanky into his pocket, "it's okay, Eve. You don't have to do it tonight if you don't want to. I know Bobby is a special friend, and you're hurting for him. I'm afraid I didn't make you feel better about it this morning."

"I was angry Mum made me come to school. But I'm glad I did. I would have only moped and cried at home."

"Well, I'm glad you did come, Eve."

The room suddenly appeared shadowy and mysterious. Yet there was something comforting in its empty desks and steadily ticking clock. Mr. Hughes was a part of it.

"Are you feeling sad, too, Mr. Hughes?"

"Bobby and . . . and his mother are very special to me. My own father died when I was a few years younger than Bobby. I guess I'm remembering how it feels . . . and how lonely."

I didn't know, and couldn't, why the thought flashed through my mind that Mr. Hughes loved Nita. It was just there, as much in my own being as I saw it in Mr. Hughes. I took a step forward.

"Mr. Hughes, I'm glad you're my teacher," I said awkwardly. "I'd like to be as good a teacher as you someday."

He smiled. "Thank you, Eve. You have a very sensitive soul. I think you'll make a very good teacher."

I threw my arms around him and hugged him, astonished that he would hug me, too. Then I turned and ran out the door, running and running before breathlessly heading for home.

5

I STOOD alone at the picture window with my flashlight. Three nights had passed, but the house at the bottom of the hill remained dark. Sighing, I flashed a lonely greeting to Boston Light before snapping off my light.

"What are you doing?" whispered a voice behind me.

I jerked around violently, nearly knocking over a lamp. Chantel stood two feet in front of me, dressed in a tight black miniskirt and carrying her shoes and coat.

"What's out there?" she asked, gazing out the window.

"Nothing," I said, holding my flashlight behind me.

"There's something. Or do you always come out here in the middle of the night and shine a flashlight out the window?"

"It's none of your business. Same as I don't ask you where you go at night."

"Evie, the things you do are just plain weird. Honestly, you give me the creeps sometimes."

"You're the creep, sneaking out of here like this."

"Say, I know what you're doing. You're sending secret messages to your Bobby love."

"I said it's none of your business."

"Yes, it is. C'mon, let me see," she insisted, tugging at my arms.

"You really want to see?"

"Yes."

"Okay, here." I held the light up and turned it full in her face.

"Ohhh!" she cried softly, her face contorting in the glare. "Turn it off!"

I snapped it off and waited for Chantel to blink away her blindness. "That was mean," she moaned. "And what do you think you're doing anyway? You'll wake up Mummy and Daddy."

"Guess you better get out of here then."

"I'm going, brat." Chantel hesitated for a moment, and then said in an apologetic voice, "Listen, I'm sorry about Bobby's dad, okay? Maybe you can tell him that for me if you want."

"If I ever see him again."

"You will. Aren't you going to the funeral?"

"Our whole class is."

"Well, he'll still be your friend, don't worry. Hey, I gotta go, okay? Promise not to tell?"

"I never do, Chantel."

Then she was gone. I could see her shadow down below on the street and the faint glow from her cigarette, dying, then flaring up again like Boston Light. A car drove up, long and sleekly dark, and Chantel quickly blended in with the silhouette at the wheel. It chugged off slowly, disappearing into the night.

I didn't see Bobby again until the day of the funeral. At the cemetery, the class stood to the side and watched the long, slow procession of cars with their headlights on entering like a dark, slithering dragon. At the head was the hearse, sleek and silver with white curtains at the windows, and in the front seat next to the driver was Bobby.

Some of the girls started to giggle. "What's Bobby doing riding in the hearse? He looks so funny."

I turned, imitating one of Daddy's glares. "How dare you laugh!"

"Girls, you know what Mr. Hughes said," Mum spoke up. "If you can't behave with dignity, you'll go straight back to school."

She clutched my hand, and I squeezed back. The girls shut up, even though they were still smiling at each other and covering their mouths with their hands.

An opaque morning mist hung over the cemetery. At one side of the narrow drive stood a small, stone chapel, green with moss. Across from it, the road circled around a large granite monument with four large American flags standing in front of it. The inscription on it read: "In memory of those who gave their lives during World War II."

Bobby's father was the first one to be buried here from Viet Nam. I wondered if they would make another monument for Viet Nam, or if Bobby's father would be the only name they would put on it.

There were many other kinds of monuments, angels with baby faces and outstretched arms, and granite urns with granite roses draped over them. Some of the grave markers had been freshly inscribed, while others were a hundred years old.

The procession turned from the monuments and lined up alongside a wide expanse of grass where several straight rows of graves were marked by tiny American flags, indicating soldiers were buried there. In a far corner of the lawn, a large, green canopy had been erected over an open grave.

Mr. Hughes made the class stand respectfully to the side of the family. He stood alone in back of us a little ways, red-faced and stern, with his hands folded in front of him, looking as solid and unbreakable as one of the granite monuments.

The early morning call of a bird broke through the stillness. We were on the curve of a hill, and even though I couldn't see the ocean, I knew it was there, just around the corner. I knew the waves were still washing up the shore, that the hazy glow above was the sun trying to burn its way through the mist, that here, somehow, the world rested from war, and there was freedom.

A golden tornado of leaves whirled across the grass. Not knowing where to look, I followed them until I saw Bobby's sad face. He was standing saluting as eight soldiers in blue dress uniforms and white hats and gloves brought his father's casket. It seemed too small for Bobby's father.

"Mum," I whispered, urgently tugging her sleeve. "How come that casket is so small? Bobby's dad could never fit in there. Is it really him in there?"

Mum frowned slightly. "Of course, it's him. Hush now." I wasn't convinced. Bobby was trying so hard to be brave, but his lower lip was trembling, and so were his hands. What if it were a horrible mistake? I held onto Mum, afraid to cry.

Nita stood next to Bobby and reached out for his hand. Her hair was twisted into a bun at the nape of her neck and covered with a black veil. A leaf, the color of her hair, brushed across her shoulder and stuck to her veil for a moment like an ornament, then blew away. I wished it had stayed, to make her look less sad.

Teeny clung to her like another leaf, her dark hair all tied up in a big blue ribbon to match her blue coat. She kept pulling Nita down to her to whisper in her ear, and then she'd look back with wide, frightened eyes at the gleaming silver casket with the striped flag draped over it.

The soldiers took the flag, folded it into a triangle, and gave it to Nita. She held it, looking down at it through her veil. Teeny anxiously reached for it. Nita leaned over so she could touch it, but straightened up again, holding the flag tightly against her. Teeny began to cry, and Nita gently cradled her head with her black gloved hand.

I looked at Bobby, and he was crying now, too. A Marine standing next to him, who looked like Bobby's father, had his arms around him. I had never seen Bobby cry before, not his whole face crying with no cap or collar to hide it. I wanted to cry, too, but I was still afraid. Afraid of what was going to change. I didn't know.

A priest began reading a psalm from the Bible, his voice trilling out the words like a stream rushing over rocks.

> I will lift up mine eyes unto the hills,
> From whence cometh my help;
> My help cometh from the Lord
> Who made heaven and earth.

I looked at Nita, her face hidden behind her veil, still looking down at the flag. I thought then about Daddy and about hating God, and it all ran together confused, on and on, like a run-on sentence.

At the end, seven Marines raised their rifles into the air and fired them three times. Their thunder boomed down the hill and reverberated throughout the entire island. I could feel it exploding inside my head each time. Teeny clapped her hands over her ears, squeezing her eyes shut at each explosion. Bobby kept still, his eyes glistening. I wondered if his dad could hear and what he thought of coming home to the sound of guns again.

We all stood still as monuments in the falling silence, crackling and ringing about our ears like distant rain.

When I walked into the kitchen after school that afternoon, Daddy was sitting at the table like a giant, wet beaver. His hair was standing in little black spikes all over his head, and his eyes were cobwebbed with tiny red threads.

I scurried past him, my head tucked low over my books. I didn't want him to touch how I felt that day, all delicate and cobwebby inside, not like the dry, broken lines in his eyes, but fragile, washed, as if with a wet morning dew.

"Well?" he said gutturally.

I paused. "Well?"

"How was it? The funeral?"

"It was sad. Funerals are supposed to be sad, aren't they?"

"Sad he died, but good thing they killed him rather than send him home with half a body."

I didn't answer him, but angrily dropped my books and ran down to the store.

Mum was busy with customers, so I started dusting shelves. The anger was building, too much so. When Mum's customers were gone, she came over and stood with her arms folded.

"Why can't Daddy ever have anything good to say?" I blurted. "I'm sick of it! Sick! Sick! Sick!" And I knocked a whole row of tomato soup cans into the aisle.

"Barbara Eve, he is sick," Mum said, calmly helping me pick up the soup cans.

"He said it's a good thing Bobby's dad died rather than come home with half a body. Bobby wouldn't care. He'd still have a dad who loved him. I don't. My daddy might as well be dead. I wish he was!"

59

"Evie, Evie, stop it!" Mum said, shaking me. She was crying, too. "It's not true, it's not true. He does love you. He just doesn't know how anymore."

I pushed Mum away and stormed out the door, sending the bells into a frenzied jangle behind me. I tore down the hill past the congregation of cars outside Bobby's house and down the steps to the beach. The tide was halfway out to the marina, leaving large, wet rocks naked in the sand. Where the waves usually made their line, the sand was smooth and hard, but past that, all the way to where the water had receded, the cold, wet sand was ridged with waves like the ocean itself.

There were no waves now. Only a mysterious, cold stillness. The water was slowly creeping forward. As if to race it, I hurried around the curve of the Cove to the rocks in front of Bobby's house. A few lights shone through the curtains, but that was all I could see.

I picked my way across the steepening rocks towards Bracken's Hill and nimbly climbed up its narrow pathway. The air was bracing and shot through me, almost taking my breath away. Overhead the sky was pale and monotonous. The sea below reflected it, a dull, winterish gray, rippling here and there with occasional whitecaps. A lone gull, searching for company, flapped in languid circles around the hill.

Boston Light blinked from the harbor. I gazed out at its penetrating light. Then I picked up a handful of rocks and began hurtling them over the cliff. The tears coursed hot and freely. I felt as if all the anger in the world were exploding inside of me. No whistling, no working could take it away — pure, straight, unrestrained anger.

"I hate God, and I hate Daddy, and I hate war, and I hate me, and I hate everything!" I screamed into the wind. "Do you hear?"

The pallor of the sky darkened, the gray seeping through it like the ocean tide across the sand. A strong gust of wind suddenly rushed up the face of the cliff and whipped across my face and bare legs. I was shivering uncontrollably, but the tears hadn't stopped yet. Boston Light blinked steadily back, brighter and brighter, her vigil soothing, almost hypnotic, until I could cry no more. I turned back towards home, but my gaze was drawn towards the white Cape Cod house where the lights behind the curtains kept another vigil, shining steadily out towards the sea.

6

Today whales are an endangered species. Too many of them have been killed so people are beginning to protect them by passing laws to make whales safe. A lot of people may not think this, but whales are important to our world. They've been around too long to just kill off. Whales are intelligent and full of mystery. People are trying to study about them now so they can learn more about life. I think people are better human beings when they try to learn about life rather than destroy it.

I put my paper down on the table and crunched into an apple. "That's as far as I've gotten."

Mum stood at the sink and peeled carrots. The kitchen was filled with the sharp odor of chopped onion and beef stew.

"Very nice," Mum said, still dabbing at her eyes that were smarting from the onions.

"I have a lot more to write," I said with a sigh, staring at the stack of library books in front of me.

"Well, I'd say you're off to a good start," Mum said, sniffing.

I put my head down on top of the paper. "Mum, I don't feel like writing any more. I don't feel like even going to school."

"I don't think it's school, Barbara Eve. I think something else is on your mind."

Tracing the bulbous figure of a whale with my finger, I tried to think exactly what it was. Winter was over, and new grass was beginning to grow over Bobby's father's grave. But other things were beginning to grow and change as well.

"It's not the same anymore," I said. "He doesn't talk to me like he used to."

"Things have changed for Bobby," Mum said quietly. "You'll see, these things take time. All you can do is be patient. I know it's hard, but time heals everything."

I slowly pushed back from the table and went to the window. Down at the bottom of the hill, the blue car was in Nita's driveway again.

"He's there again," I observed, more aloud to myself than to Mum.

"Who?"

"Him."

Mum left the sink and came over to the window. "You know, you're always looking out the window like that, like a regular little spy. Who are you watching for?"

Feeling suddenly ashamed, I let the curtain drop. "Ever since Nita went to work in that real estate place, this man from her office has been taking her out."

"Well, whatever is wrong with that? It's good she's not staying at home. She needs to make a new life for herself and her children."

"But—but it's not fair," I blurted.

"Not fair? To Bobby?"

"To Bobby. And to Mr. Hughes."

"Mr. Hughes?"

"He loves her!"

Mum's firm, thin mouth gaped wide open. "Barbara Eve, why, that is an astounding thing to say! What—how can you—who told you such a thing?"

I shrugged. "Nobody told me. I just know."

Mum leaned over me with an intense expression I'd never seen before. "Now listen to me, Barbara Eve Cooper, what you think you just know and what you imagine may be two different things, but it's not enough to base an opinion on. Who Nita sees is her very own personal business, as are Mr. Hughes's emotions, and it's not your place to make a statement about either one. I don't want you repeating what you've just said to anyone and certainly not to Bobby. I hope you haven't already."

"No. I didn't mean anything mean by it," I responded glumly.

"Of course, you didn't. But that's how rumors start, and unfortunately, there are many people in this community who love a good, juicy story."

I moved over to the sink and pulled several large, knobby carrots out of their blue plastic bag. "Can I help you, Mum?"

Mum and I didn't talk, but I could feel the tension ease as we scraped and chopped together. Life wasn't good without making things. When something ended, you had to get in there and make something new. Maybe that was what I couldn't figure out. I wanted things to be the way they had been before.

One by one, the boats began coming back to the marina in Musk Cove. The sea gulls were gathering expectantly on the beach like a crowd of anxious barterers. The water was deep blue and lapped and sang across the purply stones again.

"The whales will be coming back," I said to Bobby as we played follow-the-leader on the sea wall on the way home from school. "Every spring they start their migration back north to feed. They swim thousands of miles, even the little baby whales, and they never get lost. It's pretty amazing."

"I guess so," Bobby responded somewhat detached.

"I mean, they don't go in big pods or anything. They usually travel *alone*, or a mother with her baby. How do they know the way? It s amazing."

"They must be pretty doggone smart," Bobby said, his thoughts still elsewhere.

"I think I'm going to write a story about a whale on its journey. What are you going to do your final project on?"

"I don't know. I haven't thought about it really. Some kind of experiment, I suppose."

I stopped and looked at him. "You don't seem to be enthusiastic about it anymore."

He shrugged and jumped down onto the beach. "I guess I'm not."

I leaped after him. "Maybe, well, I was thinking . . ."

He was looking away, but I took a deep breath and continued anyway. "Well, I think it would be neat if you taught everybody the Morse Code. It has to do with electricity and light, and it would be something really different and creative."

"No," Bobby said firmly, facing me. "No, I don't want to do that."

"Why not?" I prodded him. "Because your dad taught it to you? You seem to want to forget everything about your dad. And your friends, too."

"No, I don't," Bobby said sharply.

I kicked off my shoes and socks. The sand was cool and damp between my toes, an old feeling come to life again.

"Is it him?" I asked bluntly. "He's there all the time now, but you never say much about him."

Bobby pushed the hair from his eyes and stared out across the Cove. "They're getting married."

He scooped up a few stones and began slicing them across the waves. Numb, I did the same.

"Are you serious?"

"Yeah, we had a big discussion about it last night. Bill said he knew it hadn't been a very long time and that no one could ever take Dad's place for us, but he can't help loving Mom and wanting to marry her, and she feels the same way. She says we have to go on with our lives now and that she needs Bill. So they're getting married in June. And then Mom and Bill want us to move to Florida."

"Florida?"

An icy wave seemed to wash over me. Swallowing again and again, I tried to say something else, but nothing else would come out. Everything was happening all at once again.

"B-but why do you have to move to Florida?" I finally stammered.

"It's a new start for us," Bobby said, flinging his last stone.

It skipped neatly across the crests of the waves, then disappeared.

I flung my last stone, not as smoothly or as far. "Does Mr. Hughes know?" I asked without thinking.

"Not yet." Bobby was still for a moment. "She doesn't know, but, well, I wish it was Mr. Hughes."

I stood still next to him, my heart pounding in my ears. So he knew, too. He took my hand, and I squeezed back tightly.

"I wished it too," I said almost in a whisper, not wanting to let go.

"We can write letters and stuff," Bobby said, sniffing. He wiped his nose on his arm.

"Sure."

"And we'll come back to visit."

"That would be great."

"I guess it won't be the same though."

"No." Nothing would ever be the same.

"You can have the dinghy, Eve."

I began crying, large gulps of it.

"Please don't cry, Eve. I'll come back."

He said it so assuredly, so matter-of-factly, as if he were only going away for the summer. "And we can go fishing again and go to a Red Sox game . . ."

His voice drifted off over the water, a voice that somehow wasn't his voice, but an echo of another voice.

I wiped my nose on my arm. "We can remember all the fun things, like singing with Mr. Hughes and learning the Morse Code and flashing secret messages."

He squeezed my hand again and was quiet for a moment. Then cupping his hands to his mouth, he shouted, "AND DON'T FORGET, SORRY FOR THE INCONVENIENCE!"

I took a deep breath. "SORRY FOR THE INCONVENIENCE!"

I shouted the words out over the water as loudly as I could, making myself hoarse. Then we stood together silently, breathlessly, listening hard to the clapping of the waves on the purply stones and the beckoning clink-clink of the sailless masts in the marina, telling us everything we'd heard before but could never understand.

Bobby asked everyone to bring a flashlight to school without telling them why. Mr. Hughes didn't know why either, but I did.

When Bobby stood in front of the class, he hesitated for a moment, and then said, "Since I won't be in school with you next year, I'd like to leave you something that my dad taught me. It's kind of in memory of him, but also to thank you all for your friendship to me and my family this year."

I smiled proudly at him and he smiled back. He continued more confidently, "As part of my final science project on electric current, I thought I'd teach you all something about the Morse Code. It was invented by Samuel Morse for the telegraph. It isn't used now much because of the telephone. But the military still uses a lot of codes for sending secret messages, so my dad learned the Morse Code when he was in the Marines.

"The way it was used originally on the telegraph was that through electric current, a message would be transmitted by several different kinds of taps on the transmitter. Each letter in the alphabet had a different combination of short and long taps, or what they call dots for short and dashes for long. Like *A* is one dot and one dash.

"I've made up copies of all the letters in the Morse Code for you so you can practice on your own." He passed out sheets of paper, and everybody immediately began tapping out their names on their desks. It sounded like it was hailing.

"When my dad was in the Marines, he also used the Morse Code with lights," Bobby said, his voice strong and authoritative now, causing all the tappers to look up at him once more. "It's hard, but fun once you learn it. Say you want to signal for help — S.O.S. That's three short flashes for *S*, three long flashes for *O*, then three short ones again."

He turned the lights off in the classroom, aimed his flashlight at the ceiling, and expertly launched his message. The class quickly beamed their flashlights to the ceiling and began doing the same thing. Mr. Hughes pulled the blinds down at the windows so the room became darker. The ceiling was a chaotic, jumping flood of light.

"It's better outside," Bobby said, disappointed. "That's what it was made for."

"Then let's do it outside," Mr. Hughes said. "This evening down at the Cove. Can everybody come?"

Everyone came. Even parents and neighbors came. Mum sat on the sea wall next to Nita and Bill. Bill was shy, but he was handsome with a broad smile. He treated Nita like a fairy queen. Mr. Hughes went over to talk to them and shook Bill's hand. I couldn't see his face.

We divided into two teams, and Bobby and I were captains. Bobby took his team up on Bracken's Hill while my team stayed on the beach. The air was cool, but the sky was warm and pink, with scattered purple clouds. Boston Light hadn't come on yet, but the lights of the city were beginning to sparkle across the bay like tiny diamonds on a silver necklace.

I looked over at the wall, and Mum and Nita were chattering while Mr. Hughes had his arms folded and was talking to Bill. It was as if nothing had changed or was changing. I tried not to think about it, but looked up towards Bracken's Hill, now backed by a pinkish-orange halo. A solitary beam, like a struck match, wavered from the top of the hill. Then another, and another, until the whole hilltop was covered with points of light. They began flashing in near perfect unison, S-O-S.

W-h-a-t i-s y-o-u-r l-o-c-a-t-i-o-n? I responded on my own, after my team had eagerly interpreted the message.

Bobby's single light flashed back, B-r-a-c-k-e-n-s-H-i-l-l. The blush was fading from the sky, and Boston Light suddenly blinked on. The pinpoint of light on the hill continually brightened.

W-e w-a-n-t M-r H-u-g-h-e-s, Bobby signaled.

Cheering, we jumped up from the beach. "They want you, Mr. Hughes!" we shouted.

He laughed and waved us off.

"No!" we insisted, as the light from the hill demanded again. "They want you up there!"

"Tell them I can't," he called back.

"C'mon!" we pleaded. The message from the hill came again urgently.

"Oh, go on," Nita seemed to be saying to him.

"Tell them I'm coming," he yelled, jumping down onto the beach.

H-e-s c-o-m-i-n-g! I flashed eagerly.

He climbed over the rocks and disappeared into the shadow of the hill while Bobby's team cheered vigorously. Their cries echoed across the Cove, bouncing off each rock like a song being sung in a round.

A solitary light flashed at us finally, G-r-e-a-t v-i-e-w.

We all applauded, the class and the parents and neighbors on the sea wall. On top of the hill, Mr. Hughes's silhouetted form spread out his arms and bowed.

I found out later from Bobby that Mr. Hughes had suddenly decided to accept the offer to teach music in the Berkshires. I would wonder often about his decision to leave. But what I would remember always was his silhouette bowing on the hill, the dusk changing into delicate shell-like shades of blue and lavender, and in ever-widening circles across the island and the bay and the sky the call of lights.

The
Causeway

7

EVERYTHING changed the summer Bobby left. I gave up on God and praying. I figured nothing good had come of it, so I didn't want any part of it anymore. Mum said God takes time. God took everything as far as I was concerned. But what I didn't understand then was that God changes everything, too, like the pieces of glass in a kaleidoscope, mixing them up only to make a new picture out of them.

"She's heartbroken," Mum was saying to Daddy. "She needs to do something different this summer.

"But modeling classes?" Daddy grumbled. "What's she gonna do with that?"

"Well, it's a whole course of classes, not just modeling. See, the brochure says good grooming, skin care, dance and movement, hairstyling. It will make her feel good about herself."

Daddy grumbled a few more objections. I leaned out the bathroom, trying to hear more clearly. It sounded like Mum was winning.

Looking in the mirror at my dull, thin hair, lashless eyes, and pug nose, I sighed and made a face. It was ridiculous to think I'd ever have a chance at being a model. But more than that, it was the last thing in the world I wanted to be.

It was all on account of Chantel's winning a scholarship to the Patricia Lamont Boston School of Beauty and Movement. The last week of school every year, Chantel's gym teacher invited Miss Lamont to come and give a talk about being beautiful. Then she gave a summer scholarship to her school to the student she thought would make the best model. Chantel said she would probably win, and she did.

"Excuse me," she said, sulking in the doorway. "I have to use the bathroom."

"Go ahead, Queen of the Universe."

"Do you mind?"

"I'm trying to listen to Mum and Daddy."

Chantel rolled her eyes. "It's so absurd, this whole thing," she whispered angrily. "You don't even want to go, and yet you're going to let Mum waste her money on you."

"No, I won't. I'll be working to pay her back all summer. That's the deal."

"It's still a waste if you don't want to go."

"Well, maybe I *do* want to go. Maybe it'll be fun!"

I stalked past her back to the bedroom. Anything was worth getting off the island that summer. Without Bobby, it seemed the loneliest place on earth to me. I hadn't been down to the Cove once since they'd left. Bobby had left his dinghy, but I hadn't the heart to go out in it.

I'd never gone into Boston except on field trips. It was always there, so close across the bay from Musk Cove, like the moon when it's full. I was content enough to know it was there without having to touch it.

But now, as our bus rumbled along the causeway, I felt giddy. Cut loose for the very first time. The water was a brilliant blue, its whitecaps racing boldly across the outstretched beach. Three Musk Coves could fit side by side along this expanse. On the left side of the causeway, there was no beach, only water and the curve of the mainland that led to Boston.

I pressed my face close to the window. The glass felt cool. I was already perspiring and itching in my dress. Chantel sat aloofly behind me, filing her nails. She was dressed all in white with a big, floppy white hat. When she got on the bus, she smiled and pretended she didn't know people were looking at her.

I turned around and looked at her admiringly. She really was very pretty.

"So, what's this Miss Lamont like?" I asked, wanting to talk.

"Oh, she's very tall and fashionable," Chantel said, not looking up from her nails. "She used to be a model, you know."

"Is she nice?"

"She was nice to me."

"Does my hair look okay?" I'd tried to curl it, but I could already feel it hanging limply about my face.

Chantel gave me a critical appraisal. "You need a new do."

"A new do what?"

"Maybe Miss Lamont can help you figure out a new way to wear it."

"Look, I know you're not all that excited about my coming along," I said uncomfortably. "If I don't like the classes, I may not go."

"Well, maybe it'll be good for you," Chantel said, blowing on her nails. "Besides, Daddy's such a poop, you need to get away from him."

I looked at her with a sudden longing to be close. "He didn't always used to be a poop. We used to have good times, remember? We used to visit him at the station and run wild all over the place."

It made her laugh. "Yeah. Those were good times." She went back to her own thoughts. Then she asked lightly, "You miss Bobby?"

I twisted my hands in my lap and nodded.

"You'll get over it," she said briskly. "There'll be all kinds of cute new guys at school next year."

"I'm really not interested," I said, turning back to the window. We were off the causeway and heading south to Boston. Nothing to look at now but used car lots and weather-beaten fish shanties. Soon open patches of backwater appeared with long, waving fringes of grass. The orange, corroded hull of a ship loomed up from a shipyard. Houses began appearing again, narrowly squashed together like pleats in an accordion and their colors faded from the salted air.

It was a strange, in-between nowhere world that didn't seem to connect to anything. Then suddenly we were flying high over a bridge with all of Boston sprawled in front of us. The harbor was alive with boats trailing white lines of foam behind them. Everything suddenly seemed large and polished, and Somewhere.

For a moment, I forgot I was coming here to learn how to be beautiful.

"This is where we're supposed to get off," Chantel said.

"What?" I wasn't listening. We were in a maze of red brick buildings and cars on every side.

"Here, this is where we get off." She was moving towards the door before the bus had even stopped.

I scrambled after her. "Wait up!" I demanded as she floated down the street. The thought of getting lost was terrifying. She didn't wait, so I ran madly after her. "How do you know where to go?" I said, breathlessly catching up.

"I'm no dummy. I have exact directions." She waved a piece of paper in front of me. Then we marched up one side street and down another.

"I thought you said you knew where you were going," I said after the third zigzag.

"I do, now be quiet." She stopped to study her piece of paper, then stalked off back the way we'd come.

"Maybe we should ask for help," I suggested.

Chantel didn't like suggestions, least of all mine. Pretending she didn't hear me, she made me trot another two blocks behind her before waltzing up to a man in a business suit.

"You're on it," the man said crisply after she asked him about the street.

"Oh." Chantel backtracked again. Irritated, I followed less enthusiastically this time. It was no fun running around in a dress and patent leather shoes.

Chantel stopped at the end of the street and looked up. Then she looked back to see where I had gone and put her hands on her hips. "Are you com-ing? This is it!"

It seemed an out of the way place for a beauty school. Wedged in between a camera store and ice cream parlor was an elegant pink and black sign: THE PATRICIA LAMONT BOSTON

SCHOOL OF BEAUTY AND MOVEMENT. Behind the large glass window was a carpeted room surrounded by mirrors. Some girls in party dresses were sitting in chairs lined up in rows. None of them looked like a Patricia Lamont.

"Now," Chantel said in a warning voice, "DON'T do anything dumb, okay?"

"I'm already doing something dumb," I muttered. "This is the dumbest place I ever saw."

"Well, go home then."

"Mum would kill you."

"Look, let's try to make a good impression, okay? I may get some modeling contacts out of this."

Whistling, I gave the ice cream parlor a hungry glance and reluctantly followed Chantel into the mirrored room. All the girls looked up when she made her entrance. They smiled half-frozen smiles, then looked away. There was no escaping the mirrors. My hair was as wilted as a dead lettuce leaf, reflecting back at me everywhere I looked.

"Where is Miss Lamont?" Chantel wondered aloud.

"She went back to her office," one of the girls said, giving Chantel a stiff lookover. "She'll be right back."

There wasn't anyone there my age. All the girls had bouffant hairdos and inch-thick makeup. I sat down in the front row next to Chantel since those were the only seats left. Whistling softly, I slunk low in my chair, wondering why I had ever thought this might be fun.

"Beautiful ladies do NOT whistle!" A giant Barbie doll in a tight pink dress was standing in the back doorway, glaring at me. "Beautiful ladies do NOT slouch!"

Appalled, I shot up in my chair ramrod straight.

"Girls, girls," she said in a wispy voice, "I see posture and bad habits are going to be first on our list." With perfect posture, she pivoted into the room with quick, tiny steps. Her white blonde hair looked like an atom bomb had exploded in it, and every feature of her face was painted porcelain smooth. It was hard to believe she was real.

Chantel turned to her adoringly and held out her hand.

"Hello, Miss Lamont. I'm Chantel Cooper from Emerson High School."

Miss Lamont took her hand, and her mouth turned into a round, red cherry. "I'm *soooo* glad you were able to make it. Girls, this is Chantel Cooper. Doesn't she look absolutely *exquisite!* Now who is our other new girl? I don't recall meeting you, dear."

"Eve Cooper," I said dismally.

"What was that, dear? Speak up. I see some voice training is in order here, too."

"*Eve Cooper!*" I nearly shouted.

"She's my sister," Chantel explained apologetically. "She came along to see if she might like to take some classes, too."

"Well," gurgled Miss Lamont, "isn't that nice. And what a wonderful example you are for her to follow!"

I waited until Miss Lamont turned away and Chantel was looking at me. Then I stuck my finger in my mouth, pretending to gag myself.

"Now, girls," Miss Lamont said, her eyelashes batting up and down like little black fans, "I'm going to pass out paper and pencils, and I'd like you to list the areas you're most interested in improving in yourself."

"Like what?" asked a girl.

Miss Lamont opened up a magnificent smile. "I want you to think of the *possibilities,* girls. You are here to learn the *essence of womanhood,* not just makeup and hair styling, good grooming, and modeling skills, *although* those are important skills to acquire as ladies of beauty. You are here to become a better *person.* Now what skills do you need most? It seems Miss Eve Cooper could benefit greatly from learning better posture and more ladylike habits. Perhaps you need to watch your diet, although I don't think any of you here have that problem! Whatever you think you need, put it down, put it down. We are here to learn the *essence of womanhood!*"

She handed out a batch of pink papers and pink pencils with pink-tipped erasers. Pink was her favorite color, apparently.

I chewed on my pencil while I tried to think of what I needed to learn the essence of womanhood besides better posture and more ladylike habits. Then I discovered all the girls were looking at me and giggling. Afraid of being lectured about chewing on pencils, I quickly began writing. I was going to write about having lettuce-leaf hair, but something else came out instead.

> *I do not plan on ever being beautiful, so I'm not worried about what I need to become this way. I don't think people become better or beautiful by learning it in a school like a bunch of poodles. It's something that happens inside you, not outside.*

I knew she'd think that was weird. I was about to erase it when she scooped it up and neatly patted it into the stack with the others.

"Thank you, girls," Miss Lamont said with her magnificent smile again. "I'd like to read these quickly so we can see what interests we have in this group."

Horrified, I thought of leaving then and there and waiting for Chantel in the ice cream parlor. But I was too frozen to move an inch.

"I would like to learn makeup and hairstyling . . . I want to be a model and need to know how to get started . . . I have skin problems and need to take better care of my skin . . ." She read them through breezily and for a moment, I thought she'd skipped mine. But it was the last one in the stack.

> *I do not plan on ever being beautiful, so I'm not worried about what I need to become this way. I don't think people become better or beautiful by learning it in a school like a bunch of poodles . . .*

The girls began snickering. Except Chantel. From the front mirror, I could see her face was hot and red.

"Well, now," Miss Lamont said with perfect composure, "I

79

think we are all aware that beauty is *not* skin deep. But how can we feel beautiful *inside* if we don't look our best *outside? I think this girl needs to improve her self-image, and that's why we're all here, isn't it? Remember, attitude is the key* to the essence of womanhood.

"Today, girls, we'll learn how to perfectly apply our makeup and practice different hair styles," she said, beckoning us to follow her behind all the mirrors to the makeup room. It looked like a theater dressing room illuminated by a dazzling arcade of light bulbs. There were boxes of multicolored eye shadows and rouges lining the counter and three Styrofoam heads wearing wigs.

"Wigs and hairpieces can greatly enhance your looks, and we'll learn how to experiment with them. I think to start off, we should have a mini-demonstration. Eve, you're not wearing any makeup. Why don't we begin with you?"

"Me?"

Chantel gave me a sharp elbow. "Go on!" I couldn't tell whether Miss Lamont was being sincere or trying to make fun of me. I couldn't read anything in a face like that.

"Yes, come sit right here," she said, patting the seat of a swivel-type chair.

Reluctantly, I sat down in it. She began fluffing up my hair, saw it was hopeless, and covered it up with a net.

"How old are you, Eve?" she asked, bending down into my face. Close up, I could see tiny lines all around her eyes and cracking through her forehead. She was wearing a heavy, flowery perfume, and her breath smelled like cough drops.

"Twelve," I answered her.

"Then I'd say you're ready to start learning something about makeup. You're really never too young, you know, to start good habits. First, I'm going to cleanse and moisturize your face and apply makeup. Then we'll see what we can do with your hair."

Her hands were soft but cold on my face. The girls all watched intently as she talked and continued patting my face. I couldn't see what she was doing, but only knew it was making me more and more nervous the longer she patted and poked.

Suddenly, she brought out a tube of glue and a pair of eye-lashes.

"I don't like those," I said, panicking.

"Every girl should learn how to apply false eyelashes," she said breezily. "You're going to be amazed at what they'll do for you. You have very short eyelashes, you know."

"But what if I can't get them off?"

The girls snickered. Miss Lamont ignored me and glued them on anyway. Then she whipped out a pot of rouge and a stubby orange lipstick and went to work on the rest of my face.

Whirling me around in the chair, she proudly showed me off. I frowned into the mirror. Now I looked like all the other girls, except that I looked like a twelve-year-old with an overdose of makeup.

"Now your hair is frightfully thin," Miss Lamont went on, moving over to the wigs. "Have you ever thought of trying a wig?"

There was more snickering, louder this time, and I began to feel ill. They *were* making fun of me. This was all a big joke.

Miss Lamont lifted a soft, curly blonde wig off one of the heads and planted it on me. It wasn't bleached and wild like her hair, but more natural, almost the color of Nita's hair. She arranged and combed it, but it still looked like a wig to me. I didn't look like me anymore, that was for sure.

"Well, what do you think, girls?" Miss Lamont asked. "Doesn't Eve look much more feminine and grown-up?"

Chantel looked shocked. No one dared laugh now. Miss Lamont was dead serious.

I hopped off the chair. "I think I look like a grown-up midget!" I declared.

"There's *nothing* wrong with the way you look!" Miss Lamont said, suddenly angry. All the breeziness and phoniness went out of her face. "I don't like wasting my time with *anyone* who isn't willing to improve herself. I see you're not going to fit in here."

"Fine, then. Good-bye!"

Stung with humiliation, I headed blindly for the door while

Miss Lamont and the girls watched me go, too surprised to say anything. Perhaps they thought I would come back. No one said a word or came after me. I rushed out into the Boston sunlight, forgetting who I was or where I was going, taking all of Miss Lamont's essence of womanhood with me.

8

THE FARTHER I walked away from Miss Lamont and her famous School of Beauty, the more I decided I never wanted to see Chantel or home again. I'd had enough. Somehow I'd find a way to Florida and live with Nita and Bobby and never have to mess with this place again. Thoughts and plans began clacking through my mind like an accelerating steam engine.

First, I needed money. I caught a glimpse of myself rushing by in the shop windows and stopped for a moment. A stranger stared back. *I did look a little* older, I thought critically, *old enough to get a waitressing job maybe.*

A small lunch counter on the corner had a sign in the window, HELP WANTED. It was a dingy, greasy place that didn't look as if they would be particular about the sort of help they could get. I took a deep breath and confidently walked in.

A woman with a pile of red curls on top of her head was mopping up the counter. She had two black penciled-in eyebrows that looked like caterpillars crawling across her forehead. She handed me a menu with something red like ketchup crusted on the edges.

"Uh," I said, coughing and trying to lower my voice, "I'd like to apply for a job. I saw your sign."

The woman didn't stop, but kept bustling around the counter. "How old are you, deah?" she asked casually.

I wasn't sure how old was old enough. "Uh, sixteen," I ventured.

This time she stopped her bustling and stood in front of me with her hands on her hips. "Sixteen, huh? You don't look sixteen."

"Well, I'm kind of small for my age."

"You runnin' away from home, is that it?"

I swallowed hard. "I've had experience with cash registers. I mean, I've worked in a store so I have work experience."

"Look, deah, I don't care what you can do. You ain't sixteen, and I don't hire runaways."

She turned her back to me, and the interview was over. Determined, I marched out and tried a doughnut shop next, then another lunch counter, then a drugstore, then everything and anything, until Florida began looking like an impossible dream.

"Well, I'll find a way somehow," I muttered. "I'm going to Florida, and nobody can stop me."

I came to the end of the street and was suddenly at the edge of the Boston Common. A huge demonstration was going on. The park was packed with young people dressed in jeans and beads and wearing twisted bandanas around their long, flowing hair. They were sitting on the grass and around the fountains. They held large, crudely drawn peace signs and signs that read END VIET NAM NOW and MAKE LOVE, NOT WAR. Surrounding them on the fringe were a number of scowling, big-bellied policemen.

I had never seen such a gathering except on television. Nervously, I crossed the street and skirted around the crowd to the other side of the Common. Across the walkway away from the confusion behind me was a street different from all the rest. The sidewalks were made of red brick and instead of old, dingy shops, they were lined with artists' galleries and antique shops. *Maybe I'd have some luck here,* I thought, feeling hopeful again.

I stopped and gazed in a window with an enormous seascape perched on a miniature easel. There was a light fixed over it so that the tops of the waves gleamed almost transparently, as if it were really the sun, not a light bulb shining on them.

I pressed closely to the window so that all I could see were the blue-green waves with the light shining through them, trying to make the magic real. It worked for a second, then was lost. As

I wandered on, I found seascapes in more windows, but I didn't think any of them were quite as grand as the first.

Sandwiched in between an antique store and bookshop was a small courtyard sunk below street level. In the courtyard stood a fountain with a baby angel pouring water out of a fish's mouth. A myriad of brightly colored pots filled the courtyard and surrounded the fountain like a collection of rare and wonderful stones.

Entranced by the color and tranquility of it, I slowly made my way down the few steps into the courtyard and over to the open door. A hand-painted sign read: THE CHARLES STREET POTTERY.

The fountain and shade of the courtyard created a soothing coolness. Inside the shop, it was even cooler. A man with long, sandy hair was intently creating something on a potter's wheel. He was too absorbed to look up. But I thought maybe part of the absorption was the music rushing and flowing around the small shop like the purest water there ever was.

It was unlike any music I'd ever heard. I stood numb, wanting it to go on forever. It seemed to be the music of the sea itself, cresting and racing, as if to shore, running along purply stones, then rushing whimsically out again. But it was far more than whimsical. It went deep, deep down, like the song of a solitary whale, lonely and full of life all at once, aching with more sadness and beauty than I thought I could contain.

When it was over, the potter looked up, twice, as if he didn't quite believe what he was seeing. His young, handsome face was tanned, and it crinkled around the eyes. His beard and moustache were darker than his hair. Suddenly, a gleaming, white smile broke through all that hair and warmed me all over.

"Hi!" he said with a small, startled laugh.

Feeling extremely self-conscious, as if someone other than myself had been standing there a moment ago, I could only nod.

"How are you?" he asked.

I shrugged awkwardly, somehow not wanting to leave.

"Why don't you come in?" he invited. "I'm just getting ready to throw another pot."

"What was that music?" I heard myself breathe, wondering if he heard me.

"Rachmaninoff. Piano Concerto no. 2. Do you like classical music?"

"I liked that."

"I like it a lot myself. What did you like about it?"

I shifted uncomfortably and scratched at the back of my wig. "I don't know. It reminded me of the ocean, I guess."

"It kind of builds and swells and tears down all your defenses, doesn't it? Purifies you in a way?"

I nodded, terrified suddenly that I was going to cry.

"Well, don't just stand there. Come inside!"

I moved towards him, away from the shadows of the door and courtyard. Inside, the shop was filled with pots of every shape and size, some finished and glazed to a polished shine, others still gray and wet. The damp earthy smell of clay permeated the air. Its dust was everywhere, on the floor and workbenches and potter's wheel. The wheel itself sat like an island in the middle of the room.

"My name's Mike," the potter said, looking straight into my eyes. His were blue-green eyes, like the colors in the seascape.

"I'm Barbara Eve Cooper," I said, trying to sound sixteen again.

"Barbara Eve, pretty name. It's a pleasure to meet you!" Then he laughed. It was the heartiest, most musical laugh I had ever heard. He searched my face thoroughly as if greatly puzzled, and then laughed again. It was the kind of laugh that erased any kind of gloom in you, but I was too startled by it to feel anything but uncomfortable.

"What's so funny?" I demanded.

"I'm sorry, really, how rude of me. I wasn't laughing at you. I mean, I'm not often visited by charming young ladies."

"I'm, well, sort of looking for a job in case you're wondering why I'm all dressed up," I said nervously.

Something like a signal clicked on in Mike's eyes. "I see. Well, what kind of a job are you looking for?"

"Oh, anything, really. I'm mostly good at working in stores. I'm very good on a cash register."

"I'm sure you are. Well, I'm afraid I don't have any cash registers. I pretty much work by myself."

"Oh, that's okay. I didn't come in here looking for a job. There were just so many pretty things . . ." I looked about the room wistfully. It would be nice to work in this kind of place. It was a whole new world.

"Have you ever seen a potter work before?"

"No, never."

"Well, watch carefully then."

The wheel spun magically in front of me. In its center, Mike had thrown a small lump of clay. His hands, strong, yet gentle, closed over the lump. Spinning the wheel faster, he leaned his body forward, bearing all his weight against the clay. I thought he would crush it flat, but then he lifted his hands off. The lump had turned into a pointed, upside-down cone, like a miniature pyramid.

"How'd you do that?" I asked, amazed.

"It's the wheel. Watch."

He scooped up a handful of water from a basin next to him and drizzled it over the cone. With a precise movement of his middle finger, he made an indentation in the top of the pyramid. Suddenly, it opened up, not just the top but the whole piece of clay, into a spinning cylinder. In an instant, Mike pulled the clay up with his fingers, as if he had sprung loose a tight coil. Up and down his hands continued, gliding with the clay as if the pot were really making itself. I saw it was going to be a vase. Every movement was perfect. The clay, the wheel, and Mike's hands flowed like the music, like water, like everything that is meant to be beautiful together.

The wheel stopped, and Mike ran a wire string under the base of the vase. Then he pulled it off on a round disk attached to the wheel and set it down on a table next to several other freshly thrown pots.

"Do you like it?" he asked, meaning the vase.

I nodded my head, meaning the whole of it, the wheel, the clay, the magic.

"I wish I could do that," I said, taking a deep breath. "Is it hard?"

He laughed his deep, full-bodied laugh. "It took me years. Looks easy, doesn't it? Nothing beautiful comes easy, remember that."

I watched him throw another vase, then a curved bowl, trying hard to understand that same crushing, gliding movement that made the clay respond and spring so quickly to life. He never missed a beat. But trying to capture it in my mind was futile. It was as elusive as the music. A woman's operatic voice had come over the radio now, but still the strange, haunting and inexpressible beauty of the piano concerto filled me. Unable to be still any longer, I wandered around the shop, touching the glossy smooth surfaces of vases, bowls, and teapots whose radiant colors reminded me of the purply stones on the beach and the iridescence of fish under water.

"Why are you looking for a job?" Mike asked in a gentle voice. With his gentleness, all the defenses suddenly came tumbling down. I stood in a corner, unable to answer because I was crying. "Barbara Eve?" His voice was soft and close behind me. "If you'd like to tell me, I'd like to hear about it."

"You must think I'm pretty ridiculous," I sobbed.

"Anyone who falls in love with Rachmaninoff and says it reminds her of the ocean is someone I take pretty seriously," he said.

I slowly turned around, mumbling and hiccuping, and then I told him the whole story—about Bobby and his dad, the beauty school, and Miss Lamont.

He listened intently, offering me his clay-smudged hanky and encouraging me on in a way that I knew everything had to be the truth with him.

"I was going to tell you I was sixteen," I said, biting my lip, "but I don't suppose you'd believe me."

He laughed again, only gentler this time, and shook his head. "Barbara Eve, Barbara Eve. *You* are a very special little girl under this mask of yours. I want you to go take this mop off your head and wash your face back to normal so I can meet the *real* Barbara Eve Cooper."

"She's rather plain," I said reluctantly as he motioned towards the curtain.

"I doubt that." He was smiling.

"She has stringy, yucky hair, I'm warning you."

In the back of the shop behind the curtain was where Mike lived, I discovered. It was a small, rather dark room with an unmade bed in one corner and a table, chairs, sofa, and record player crowded together in another. Along one wall was a sink, stove, and refrigerator, all covered up with dirty dishes, pots, and pans. Something soft rubbed up against my leg and purred.

"Nice kitty," I murmured, leaning down to pet her. She followed me into the bathroom and jumped up on the back of the toilet to watch me.

It was a dingy, windowless closet with a shower and no tub. The place was filthy, I decided with disgust. I peeled off the wig with an enormous sense of relief and hung it on the doorknob. Then I peeled the eyelashes off, lash by lash.

Since there was still some stickiness to them, I tried pasting one to the mirror. Giggling, I stuck up the other one, and taking the soap, drew a smiling face underneath them.

"What do you think, kitty?" The cat cocked her head, jumped down, and began pawing at the door.

"Just a minute." I vigorously washed my face, harder than I'd ever washed it in my life. There weren't any towels, so I used the bottom of my skirt for drying.

Nothing could be done for my squashed hair, but at least it was mine again. Taking a deep breath, I stepped back into the pottery shop with my flat hair and scrubbed face and wet skirt. Suddenly, I felt at home.

Mike was still sitting at his wheel. He looked up, and a smile like the sun broke across his face. "Now you look real. Don't ever let anybody do that to you again! Come here."

The sea-blue eyes gazed searchingly again into my own for a moment. "You know what I see, Barbara Eve?" he said.

"What?"

"I see a little girl who is going to grow up to be quite a remarkable lady."

"How do you know?"

"Because I wouldn't say it if I didn't."

The cat had followed me and was rubbing against my legs again. I stooped down to pick her up, and she tilted her neck back to be scratched.

"You've made a friend for life," Mike warned.

"I like her. What's her name?"

"Beethoven. Not very feminine, but I didn't know until she had kittens. Only one lived though. Mozart's around here somewhere. He's the one with the wild look in his eyes."

I laughed. "Do you just, well, except for Beethoven and Mozart, do you live here all alone?"

"Except for Beethoven and Mozart, I live here all alone," Mike responded with his laugh full and bright again.

"I like it here," I said, cradling Beethoven who was purring ecstatically. "It's sort of a mess though. Maybe you could use some help."

Mike threw back his head and laughed so hard I could only laugh back.

"It's not funny!" I shouted finally.

He shook his head, still laughing. "Do you know what I am, how poor I am? You're right. This place is a mess. But I'm a potter. I live, breathe, and sometimes eat this clay. I don't think you'd like this kind of life."

"I don't care. I think it's beautiful here. I told you, I'm not going back home again."

"Barbara Eve, you know you can't run away. Your family needs you and you need them. Running away isn't the answer anyway." I pressed my cheek into Beethoven's fluffy neck.

"Well, what is?"

"I'm working on that answer myself," he said with a soft seriousness to his voice. "Look, I'll tell you what. If you promise me you'll go home, the next time you're in Boston, come see me and I'll teach you something about clay. How's that?"

A wave of joy swelled up inside me, then rushed out again.

"But how can I come back here if I go home? Mum will know I quit the school, and she won't let me come here by myself."

Mike frowned. "You're right. That is a problem. Besides there's too much restlessness in the Common these days. You shouldn't be wandering around by yourself, Barbara Eve."

I scratched Beethoven's neck once more. "Well, I'll think of something. I guess I better go find my sister before she leaves and the gig's up."

"Well, let me walk you back."

"But what if somebody comes in your shop?"

"It's my shop. I can close it for a few minutes."

He took me back down Charles Street in long, sauntering strides, with his hair waving behind him like some kind of flag. He could have easily fit in with the masses of people camped out on the Common, except that looking up into his face, I saw something different there. Something from the deep, lonely, beautiful, and brave, like the music, and I wondered what it was.

9

"Why did you act that way? You embarrassed me in front of everybody."

Chantel had found me camped out in the ice cream parlor with all of my lunch money spent on a jumbo hot fudge sundae. I calmly slurped up the rest of it while she finished her tirade.

"I had to apologize to Miss Lamont for my weird little sister; how do you think that felt? You really insulted her *and* me. I can't believe I ever let Mum talk me into letting you come. You, you little pig, you've got chocolate on your dress!"

I looked down. Sure enough. One long dark dribble. I ignored it and kept on slurping.

"What's the matter with you? You're not listening to a word I'm saying! What did you do with Miss Lamont's wig?"

I'd completely forgotten about it. "I'm listening if you're done yelling," I said.

"Where's the wig?" Chantel's face was as livid as her voice.

"Don't worry, I'll get it back."

"You'll get it back?"

"Look, I'm sorry I embarrassed you. But how do you think I felt? I felt totally *stupid*, that's how I felt! Miss Lamont's the biggest fake I ever saw. She wants everybody to look just like her. Well, I don't want to look like her, not even if you paid me a million bucks!"

"Just give me the wig," Chantel fumed, trying to control her voice. People were looking at us.

"I don't have it, I told you. I'll get it for you next week."

"Next week!"

I swallowed hard. "We have to make a deal. This is the deal. If you promise not to tell Mum about what happened, I can come back with you next week and get the wig."

Chantel's mouth opened to say something, but it stayed open for a few seconds before saying it. "What did you *do* with it?"

"Promise not to tell Mum *anything*?" I demanded. "I don't want to go to your modeling school. I just need to come to Boston with you. Mum would never let either one of us come on our own, anyway, so you need me to keep coming in with you."

Chantel gave an impatient little sigh. "I won't promise anything, you little fink, until you tell me where you've been all morning. You think I'm going to be responsible for letting you wander all over the place?"

"I'm going to learn pottery," I said as casually as I could, knowing I had to tell her some of the truth.

She laughed. "Pottery? Where?"

"At a pottery shop. That's where I left the wig."

"You want to come in to Boston every week so you can run off and take pottery lessons? Why can't you tell Mum that?"

I fidgeted and spilled more chocolate on my dress. "You know Mum. She wouldn't let me go off by myself."

"You're a disgusting mess. Come on, we have to catch the bus."

"Is it a deal?" I trotted out the door and up the street after her, trying to keep up again.

"Why don't you take pottery lessons somewhere else?"

"Because, because this potter's my friend. And I don't have a friend right now. Please, Chantel."

She turned and looked at me, but without any anger this time. I didn't know how to read the expression in her eyes. It was too distant and unseeing. "Okay, Evie, I won't tell," she said with a somewhat exasperated edge to her voice. "But if you get in trouble, I'm telling Mum exactly what happened today. I won't know anything about pottery lessons, understand?"

"I won't get into trouble," I assured her with excitement. I could suddenly hear the music again.

Something different was on the radio when I walked into his shop the next week. It was a light and dancing kind of music, not rock, but something that butterflies would dance to. He looked up from his wheel and laughed as if I'd surprised him all over again.

"Barbara Eve! You got away with it, did you?"

"Chantel and I made a deal." I came quietly to his side and basked in the warmth of his smile. "I don't tell her secrets, so she can't tell mine."

He was putting the finishing touches on a vase on the wheel. I watched silently as he deftly removed it and set it on a shelf to dry along with a dozen others he'd already thrown that morning.

"You mean this is going to be a clandestine relationship?"

"What's that?"

"Secret and illegal."

"It's the only way I can get here. I'm sure as heck not going back to beauty school!"

Mike's laughter rang out like a church bell, filling the shop. "No, that would be brutal. I'm glad you could come back, Barbara Eve."

"They're not so crazy out in the Common today. So, you see, I'll be perfectly safe."

"Things have calmed down a bit this past week, but that doesn't mean it won't get crazy again."

"Mike, I won't get hurt," I said with confidence, happy just to have found him again.

"So," he said, "you've come to learn about pottery?"

"You bet! But can I change my clothes first?" I'd brought jeans and t-shirt in a gym bag. "You know, I left the wig here," I said, suddenly remembering. "I'm supposed to give it back."

Mike frowned. "Oh, I'm afraid I have bad news about that. Mozart found it and got a little overly friendly with it. Well, not friendly exactly. More like excited!"

I gaped in horror. "You mean, he *ate* it!"

"Just about. There were curls all over the place. You should have seen him when I found him. He had this little curl hanging over his lip like a goatee."

He looked so helpless and forlorn about it, I burst out laughing. "What will I ever tell Chantel? She'll kill me!"

"I'm sure it can be replaced. Find out how much it cost, and I'll reimburse you."

He smiled; then he laughed, deep and uproariously. And I laughed even harder, harder than I could remember, until my stomach hurt and tears ran from my eyes.

"I think Miss Lamont deserved it actually," he said, wiping his own eyes. "Mozart took revenge for you, so you're all taken care of."

I took my gym bag behind the curtain, and then peeked out again. "Mike?" I said, smiling widely.

"What?"

"You're fun to laugh with."

He laughed all over again, and I let the curtain drop. Beethoven promptly appeared and nuzzled my legs as if she too was glad to see me. I reached down to scratch her between the ears.

"So, where's this crazy kid of yours, huh? Where's Mozart?"

I rapidly changed into my jeans, surveying the tiny apartment.

Nothing had changed since last week. I poked my head back through the curtains.

"I'm going to work in here!" I announced loudly.

"What?"

"You need help *bad*!"

I started with the dishes. Then I scrubbed off the grease and dirt coating the countertops and stove. The table came next. I made his bed and dusted the furniture. On top of the rickety table next to his bed was a picture of two soldiers in army fatigues, their arms around each other's shoulders.

I stared at it for a moment before realizing one of the men was Mike. Picking it up, I dusted the glass over and over and over again. Then I heard the curtain part and turned around to see Mike.

"It got so quiet, I thought something had happened to you," he said.

"Is this you?" I asked, holding up the picture.

"Yeah, me and Jack, my best friend. We were in Nam together."

"When were you there?"

"Three years ago."

"I didn't know you were in Viet Nam."

He came over and gently took the picture from me. "I came back, but Jack didn't make it." He set the picture down on the table and looked around the room. "Wow, it's a miracle!"

"Do you have a broom around this place?" I asked, following him back into the shop.

He pointed to one leaning against the corner near a large sink. The bristles were about shot, and I doubted I could do much with it, but I attacked the floor anyway.

"Mike, what was it like there?" I couldn't help asking. "In Viet Nam?"

"Not much fun, Barbara Eve."

"Was it terrible every minute?"

"Every minute for a year of my life. Hell couldn't be much worse."

"Do you believe in hell?"

"I do now."

"Do you believe in God, Mike?"

"Yes. But I'm not sure I understand Him anymore."

"Neither do I. I asked Him to bring Bobby's dad home and He didn't."

"I asked Him to save my friend, Jack Riley, and He didn't. I even asked Him to take me instead. But it didn't happen."

"Why, Mike?"

"I don't know, Eve. Seems to me God didn't save Jesus from dying either. He had other plans. Maybe that's the answer."

"What other plans, Mike?"

I stood and watched him work. His hands seemed so sure of

everything they did. Only the expression on his face seemed doubt-ful at times. He looked up at me, and it was with the doubting look.

"I was a law student at Harvard when the war got going. I thought I should go, so I did. When I came back, nothing was the same, nothing mattered that did before, except this interest I had in pottery. I was good at it, and someone offered me this space, so I opened up a shop. It calms me. I guess you could say I feel at peace."

"I'm sorry you lost your best friend, Mike. I've lost my best friend, too, even though he didn't die like yours."

"It's sad all the same, isn't it?" Mike said, looking at me thoughtfully.

He stood up and took the broom from my hands and led me over to a large vat of wet clay. Digging in, he scooped up a hand-ful and pressed it into my hands.

"Are you ready to learn something about pottery?" he asked. I held the damp, pungent clay as if it were a brick of gold. "You have to learn the feel of the clay first," he instructed, leading me over to a worktable. "To begin with, the clay has to be wedged and made into a ball. Wedging is to get all the air bubbles out so the pot doesn't crack later on when it's fired. It's kind of like kneading bread dough, if you've ever done that. Don't fold it. Use the heel of your hand and push."

The clay was hard under my palms, but giving. Its texture felt cool and soothing, and immediately I understood its effect. I rolled and pushed it until my arms ached. Then I molded it into the ball that would become a pot.

I brought it proudly to Mike. "Now what do I do?"

"Do whatever you like with it."

Disappointed, I frowned. "What do you mean?"

"You're not ready for the wheel yet. I said you have to learn the clay first. Make your own creation just with your hands."

"You mean, make a pot?"

"Whatever you like."

I kept rolling the clay round and round inside my hands, not at all sure of what he meant. Then I began pinching and poking with my thumbs and forefingers until I formed a hollow in the middle of the ball. Soon it started to look like one of the little nests I used to make out of clay in kindergarten.

"This looks real dumb," I moaned.

Mike looked over and shook his head. "You're not done with it yet."

I continued molding it, pressing the hollow wider with my thumbs, curving the sides out more as they seemed to want to go, and suddenly I saw what it would be.

"I think it's going to be some weird kind of vase," I decided, holding it up for him to see.

He smiled. "Well, progress."

"It's not very even or symmetrical or anything. But I think I like it."

"It's not supposed to be perfect. That's not the point. Perfection is never the point, remember that."

"But you're always perfect, aren't you?" I asked, standing back to admire my own dumpy little creation in clay.

"Not always, of course not. Just most of the time." He smiled broadly, his perfect, white teeth gleaming.

I stood next to him and watched with envy as he effortlessly made his lump on the wheel spring up into a perfect cylinder.

"Hey, Mike?"

"Yeah?"

"Do you think I can do that?"

"Eventually. Play with the clay today."

"I mean, is it *really* hard or pretty easy?"

"It's *really* hard. It takes a lot of practice."

I scraped up another wet lump of clay from the barrel and slammed it down on the table as I'd seen him do.

"Mike, have you ever been married or anything?"

"Nope. Not even anything."

"How come?"

"Have you?"

"Of course not. That's a silly question to ask a kid."

"So, it's a silly question to ask a grown-up."

"No, it's not. Grown-ups are supposed to be married. Kids aren't."

"Just because I'm a grown-up means I'm *supposed* to be married?"

"Well, not *supposed*. My teacher last year, Mr. Hughes, he wasn't married."

"Well, maybe some grown-ups aren't supposed to be married then."

"I seem to be making something with wings this time," I said. I brought it over for his inspection.

"Hmm," he said. "Work on that for a while. It could be interesting."

"Mike," I said after a short pause. "I seem to be asking you all these personal questions. I guess I'm just curious."

He shook his head, and his eyes were sparkling. "I don't mind, Barbara Eve. But you may not always get very personal answers."

"You're no fun," I teased.

"Well, it takes time to get to know someone, don't you think?"

"I guess. But you know a lot of personal things about me."

Mike took his foot off the pedal and the wheel spun slower and slower, gradually revealing a delicately curved bowl. "Quite actually, you know a lot of personal things about me, too."

"Well, as long as you don't mind."

"I don't mind, Barbara Eve," he said, and his eyes were sincere.

My pot seemed to be turning into some sort of a bird. Delighted with it, I continued modeling and remodeling its head and neck and wings. It didn't matter so much how it turned out. I was learning and liking the clay itself.

Suddenly, a glossy black cat glided noiselessly past my feet on his way to the door. He sat facing out, and then twisted his head and began licking himself.

"Enter Mozart the Mad Cat," Mike boomed.

I took my clay bird over to the door and crouched down. Mozart sniffed at the bird and meandered into the courtyard to take a stretch. A couple had come down the stairs and was inspecting the pottery around the fountain.

"He doesn't look like a mad cat," I said.

"He's very lazy during the day," Mike explained. "But night-time we're talking madder than a hatter."

I laughed again at the thought of it. "I wish I could see him in action. Looks like you have customers, Mike."

The wife was exclaiming over a teapot. After a few minutes, she and her husband came in to buy it.

"You do absolutely lovely work," she said. "I've never seen such beautiful glazes. Do you have another blue one? I'd like to buy two."

"I think I have one in the back. Just a minute." Mike disappeared into a back room where he had his kiln. Meanwhile Beethoven came out to inspect the customers and get scratched.

The lady and her husband wandered around the shop until Mike came back with a second blue teapot, more brilliant than the first.

"I just finished it this morning," he said.

"How gorgeous. Look, Howard. Say, do you work on commission?"

"Sure."

"I've been looking for someone to do a set of dishes for me. Could you make them for me, same color?"

"Tell me what you want, and I'd be happy to."

Mike worked up her order, and then wrapped her teapots in newspaper. Still, she didn't want to leave.

"Have you ever seen such pretty colors?" she kept saying to her husband.

They watched Mike work on the wheel for a while before finally leaving. Another couple had come down into the court-yard.

"People really like your shop, Mike," I said proudly. "I'd think you'd be a millionaire by now."

"My pottery sells," Mike said, laughing. "But I'll never be a millionaire."

I held my bird up for him to see. He took it in his hands and studied it.

"This I like," he said finally. "Set it on the shelf over there to dry."

"Then can I paint it the purply blue like the teapots?"

"Whatever you like."

"It reminds me of the purply stones on our beach. Only they fade when you bring them home. These colors won't ever fade, will they, Mike?"

"No, the glazing process sets the color for all time."

"It's like always having the sea with you," I mused, going over to place my bird sculpture on the shelf.

"Can I work on the wheel next week, Mike?" I asked eagerly.

"We'll see. Don't be in a rush about it."

The new couple came inside and began talking to Mike. Silently, I went behind the curtain and sat on the bed to look at the picture of him and Jack. Something in it was the real, personal Mike. More than the laughing potter Mike? Or equally so? Was a purply stone its real self when it was faded in your hand, or when it was wet and shining in the sun?

10

"THE HARDEST part on the wheel is raising your cylinder up," Mike said. With one forefinger at the outside base of his pot and the other inside of it, he swiftly lifted the pot from its flat, squatty shape into a tall, elegant trunk.

"But it looks so easy," I protested, eager to get at it myself. I'd been bugging him for weeks now.

"Only because you think the wheel is magic," he answered me solemnly. "It's not. I'm afraid you're going to be disappointed. Unless you have perfect control and concentration, your pot will collapse. Remember, that takes time, okay?"

I found out he was right. As soon as I stepped on the pedal and watched the wheel spin, I felt unsure of myself. I awkwardly molded my wet lump of clay into its little pyramid, squashed it down like Mike told me to, and molded again.

"It still looks kind of floppy," I sighed. "I can't control this thing."

"So who said you have to be perfect on your first try?"

Mike helped me along so that I opened the hole right, but when it came to lifting up the sides, my pot quickly wobbled out of control and caved in.

"It's drunk," I said with a groan.

Mike laughed. "See what I mean."

I started over. He guided my fingers the next time. "You have to hold your hands absolutely steady and concentrate completely. If you let go of your concentration one second, KABAM!"

I concentrated so hard, I felt my eyes crossing. This time I tore a big hole in the clay.

"Oh, I'm doing a terrible job," I moaned. "I can't even do it when you're helping me!"

"Just don't give up. Remember to think of raising the cylinder up one ring at a time."

Starting over every time meant a whole new slab of clay had to be wedged and rolled before throwing it on the wheel. It was much more tiring than I could have imagined. Yet the wet clay spinning under my palms for the first time still felt exciting. Something new and wonderful could spring out of it at any minute. I only had to learn the secret.

Mike let me experiment and work for an hour on the wheel while he painted a row of pots for firing. The paint was dull and gray, not at all the vibrant colors the kiln produced. It was just another part of the magic of turning something lifeless into something beautiful.

The clay continued to resist my efforts at controlling it. But each time Mike guided my fingers, I thought I understood it more, and so learned patience. Finally, I was able to raise the sides of the pot without his help and without collapsing the pot. It seemed such a miracle that I nearly destroyed it then and there with excitement. It wasn't at all symmetrical, and it spouted a bit like the tip of an elephant's trunk. But it stood proudly, I thought, on its own.

"I think this pot, well, has a lot of personality," Mike said, studying it closely.

"Can I keep it, Mike? Oh, please, let me keep it," I begged.

"It's yours," he said, laughing, "for all time."

He set it on the shelf to dry. The following week I painted it with the dull, mud-colored paint. After the firing, I had my crooked little pot to go with my bird, radiant as the brightest purply stone.

I didn't want to think of summer ending and school beginning. Junior high was an unpleasant enough prospect, but knowing that my trips into Boston would have to end was unendurable. A gloom had come over me and was now settling in my stomach.

When I walked into Mike's shop on the last day of Chantel's beauty classes, he was talking to a long-haired girl in sunglasses.

"Here's Barbara Eve now," Mike said, looking up brightly. "We were just talking about you. This is Valerie Porter, a faithful customer of mine."

I nodded shyly. "What were you saying about me?"

"How you were my special friend and helper and that I'm always so glad to see you."

"It's so nice to meet you, Barbara Eve," Valerie said, remaining mysterious behind the sunglasses.

She sounded sincere, but something about her bothered me. Her face was too thin and bony.

"I better be going," she said abruptly. "I'll see you tonight. Thanks for helping Mike out, Barbara Eve. You do a good job. He needs all the help he can get!"

She had a small, friendly laugh, and her dark hair reflected red in the sunlight as she walked through the courtyard. I stared after her as she left.

"Who was *that*?" I asked, turning to Mike.

"Valerie Porter."

"'I'll see you tonight'?"

"I invited her out for dinner."

"You mean you have a *date* with her?"

Mike laughed uncertainly. "Isn't that okay?"

"Well, why do you want to go out with *her*?"

"She's a very nice person, Barbara Eve. Actually, we've gone out a couple of times."

I turned my back to him, stunned. It didn't make sense. Suddenly ashamed, I lunged for Beethoven who had just padded into the shop.

"Barbara Eve? What is it?" Mike said after a few moments of silence.

"Nothing."

"That's a lie. What is it?"

"Nothing!" I said, unable to keep anger out of my voice.

His voice was very near, but I still wouldn't look at him. It was near and strong and gentle. "Does it bother you that I go out with a girl?"

I rubbed Beethoven vigorously. Her eyes were closed and her

tongue hung out slightly in pure bliss. There really was nothing I could think of saying.

"Barbara Eve, put that cat down and come here."

Trembling, I let Beethoven slide out of my arms, and with my head still down and arms folded, I moved back towards his voice. Gently, he unfolded my arms, took my hands, and brought his face close to mine.

"Why?" he asked in almost a whisper.

I shrugged. "Now that you have a girlfriend, you won't want me to come see you anymore."

"That's not true at all."

"Besides, school will be starting soon, and this will be the last time I get to come see you."

"Maybe not every week. But I won't go away, I promise. Old Mike will be your friend whenever you need him, how's that?"

I looked at him then and smiled gratefully. But the gloom, like a dark, brooding cloud, still hung inexpressibly over me. Nothing he did or said would make it go away.

"Mike, I don't feel like working today."

All I wanted to do was bury my face in Beethoven's fur and watch Mike at his wheel. After a while, I wandered outside into the courtyard, disinterested even in the clay for the first time.

I thought through things in my mind. Everything, the island, Bobby, Mum and Daddy and Chantel, all seemed so far away, as far away as a war did when I was here with Mike or when my hands were working the clay. It could be confusing, having so many different worlds about you that you weren't sure which one you belonged to. Maybe you could belong to them all, maybe you had to, but maybe one world was the safest and most beautiful.

Mike came outside after a while and looked at me with one of his puzzled expressions.

"This really upset you, didn't it?"

"I don't know," I said, suddenly beginning to cry. "I just feel all topsy-turvy."

"Well, I guess you have a lot of things to feel topsy-turvy about, don't you?"

He leaned against the fountain and brought me to him with a strong, comforting hug.

"I'm sorry, Mike," I said, barely choking out the words. "I don't know why I feel so gloomy about everything, except that I'm going to miss being here so much."

For a moment, in broad daylight in the closeness of his arms, the gloom melted away.

Mike walked me past the teeming Common when it was time to go meet Chantel. I felt strangely calm and crumbly inside at the same time. There was a dull ache somewhere around my stomach that was unlike any ache I'd ever had. Not wanting to cry again, I hugged Mike tightly and fled without looking back.

Across the street from the usual lineup of food carts, a vendor selling hot dogs caught my eye. Suddenly famished, I crossed the street and bought a hot dog. After wolfing it down, I bought another. The ache didn't go away. Along with it came a heaviness in my head and all over my body. It was getting worse.

I took my second hot dog and wandered over to the Public Gardens across the street from the Common. Flat little boats with giant swans on the backs of them were floating around the duck pond like something out of Fairyland. I spent the last bit of my lunch money to ride one. I munched my hot dog as the driver paddled us under the footbridge and quietly around the pond. There weren't any protesters or peace signs here. Just lovers and old people on park benches and children feeding the ducks.

I thought dazedly about my summer spent with Mike, learning about clay and wheels and pots, about music and composers, and about God. I wondered if I would ever understand what he'd tried to teach me. Or if I would ever see him again.

I made my way sluggishly back to the ice cream shop where Chantel always met me. She found me with my head on the table.

"What's wrong?"

"My stomach hurts so bad, Chantel."

"Did you eat another jumbo sundae?"

"No. Just some hot dogs."

"Some? How many?"

"Two."

"Great, that's just great. Well, are you going to barf now, or can you wait till we get home?"

"I just want to go home," I moaned.

Chantel didn't walk as fast this time, but let me set the pace. She jabbered on about how Miss Lamont was going to find some modeling jobs for her this fall and even help her pick out a wardrobe.

A light dawned in the distance. "Can I come with you?" I pleaded. "I'll never get to see my potter friend otherwise."

Chantel rolled her heavily lashed eyes. "Are you in love with this guy, or what?"

"No, no, he . . ." I sighed out my last ounce of strength. "I just wish you could understand," I said forlornly.

When we got home, Mum made a big fuss about the hot dogs, turned down my bed, and fixed me some hot tea. She helped me undress, and then we noticed the funny spots on my underwear. It wasn't the hot dogs. I had been blessed with the essence of womanhood.

The
Mainland

11

A WHALE beached itself on the Cape that fall, a real one. I begged Mum to go see it, for its picture in the paper showed it sur-rounded by people, but Mum said it was too far. A massive crea-ture, it reminded me of the hull of a broken ship. The pictures showed people tying it with ropes to haul it back out to sea and hosing it down with water to keep it from dehydrating. But the whale was sick, the paper said, and probably would die no mat-ter what people did for it.

I cut out the picture and the article and put them in my whale scrapbook from last year's science project. Then I climbed up Bracken's Hill to think about it for a while. Sitting in the crisp autumn breeze, I wondered why the whale was sick and if beaching itself was just its way of dying. But why come to the land when its home was the sea? Why not die out there and let the sea bury it instead of having all these people fuss over it? Perhaps it was too tired of the journey to swim anymore and had just drifted in on the current.

It filled me with sadness and reminded me of the music again. I wished I could talk to Mike about it. He would know the reason or at least have a good reason of his own. How I missed the laughter and the music and the feel of the clay. I missed him, even more than Bobby.

I had only received one letter from Bobby. I had read it and reread it so many times I knew it by heart.

Dear Eve,

*How are you? I am fine. Mom, Teeny, and Bill are fine, too.
It's pretty hot down here in Florida. We live on a golf course
and lagoon with alligators. We also have a swimming
pool!!! Bill takes me fishing. He's a neat guy, really. I guess I
like Florida. How's your summer going?*

Love, Bobby

I'd written him a letter about Mike and the pottery I was
making. But how could I tell him what was changing inside me,
how it frightened me, and how lonely I felt? How could I tell him
I was different now? Perhaps he was different, too.

If there was a way to get back to Boston, I hadn't found it
yet. Chantel hadn't gotten any modeling jobs yet, except for
underwear ads, and Mum said, "Over my dead body."

I thought of just skipping school and taking the bus in, but
it was an all-absorbing school I was going to on the mainland
now. Every hour a bell would ring, and the classrooms would
erupt with kids shoving and yelling their way up and down the
stairs like rats to get to the next class before the second bell rang.
I was constantly terrified of being crushed, getting lost, losing
my mind, or all three.

I had a music class at the end of the day, and we sang songs
like "Red River Valley" and "Swing Low, Sweet Chariot" out of
a folk-song book with ten other kids' names in it. The books were
dog-eared and torn, and some had dirty words penciled into the
songs. I asked Mr. Herron, our music teacher, who had hair
growing out of his nostrils and none on his head, if we could listen to Rachmaninoff some day. "We might," he said thoughtfully
as if I'd asked too grown-up a question. But we were still singing
the folk songs.

Jimmy crack corn and I don't care,
Jimmy crack corn and I don't care,
Jimmy crack corn and I don't care,
My master's gone away.

I lay on my back, singing slowly and softly to the gulls over-head. They peered down at me curiously as I waved my arms up at them. "No handouts today, bud. And I don't care. And I don't care. My master's gone away."

I wrote Mike a letter about the whale, and I wrote Bobby about the whale, too. Bobby wrote a second letter saying how sorry he was to miss the whale, but he'd been to the Everglades and seen some alligators there.

I didn't mail the letter to Mike though. I was afraid he wouldn't answer it.

"You'll get over him," Chantel said in our room one night. She picked up my bird and crooked little pot that I'd set next to my collection of dried-out purply stones.

"Put them down," I ordered, looking up from the book I wasn't reading.

She looked them over curiously, and then set them back on the shelf. "I'm not going to break them," she said, offended.

"Just keep your mitts off them."

Folding her arms, she fell back on the bed and sighed. "So tell me more about this mystery man."

"I already told you about him."

"He must be pretty cute. You know, I never breathed a word to Mum."

"I appreciate it."

She lay back dreamily on the bed and began playing with her hair, twisting it and braiding it, the way she always did when she started telling me about her love affairs.

"You know, my drama teacher, Mr. Peters, is awfully cute. I think I'm going to try out for the drama club this year. He asked me to, and—" She began giggling.

I slammed my book shut. "I'm going to the kitchen."

113

She sat up and swung her long legs over the side of the bed. "You'll get over him, Evie," she called after me.

Chantel couldn't carry a tune if her life depended on it, but she got the lead in the senior class fall musical. Mr. Peters said they would dub her voice with someone else's behind the curtain. Chantel was Queen of the Universe again. I should have suspected. But Chantel hadn't told me anything this time.

Cindy Ferelli and Erin Smith were swapping lipsticks in the girls' locker room when I walked in. They stopped immediately and began staring with large, curious eyes.

"Isn't Chantel Cooper your sister?" Cindy asked. Cindy's older sister, Chris, had been homecoming queen at the high school. Cindy wanted to be everything her sister was. She was already the most popular girl in seventh grade.

"Yes, why?" I asked guardedly.

Cindy tilted her face slightly, and her eyes became cold and ready to hurt. She snapped her gum. "Do you know she's fooling around with the drama coach? That's why she got the lead in the musical. My sister should have gotten the part. She can sing, and your sister can't."

"You're lying!" I snapped back, even though I knew it was the truth.

Unruffled, Cindy and Erin kept staring. Erin was the second most popular girl in seventh grade, but only because she did every thing Cindy did. "They've already been caught, so everybody knows," she said smugly.

"They got caught last night after rehearsal," Cindy quickly broke in. It was her story. "And now it's probably a big scandal, and they're going to fire Mr. Peters."

"That's not true!" Quivering with anger, I turned and marched out of the locker room, not knowing where to go, but it wasn't going to be gym class. Other girls were brushing past me, staring, as if the whole world knew.

Chantel came home late that night from play practice as usual. I lay awake until I heard the door shut and her soft tiptoeing down the hall. She didn't turn on any light when she came in but shuffled around in the darkness. I watched her shadow for a few moments, and then sat up and turned on the bedstand lamp.

"You're awake," she gasped in a small voice.

In the closeness of the room, she looked like a wild woman. I knew she hadn't been to any play practice. Her makeup was smeared all over her face, and her hair was a tangled, flowing rat's nest.

"Why are you home so late?" I demanded.

"What are you, my mother?" she said, beginning to undress.

Just then Mum's hoarse call came down the hallway. "Chantel?"

"Yes, Mum," she said, quickly snapping off the light.

"Did everything go all right?"

"Yes, Mum. I'm going straight to bed."

Mum's shadow appeared in the doorway. "I got a call from the principal today. He wants to see me. Well, I couldn't possibly drop everything and go today. It sounded urgent. What's happened, Chantel?"

"Can we talk about it in the morning, please? It's . . . it's my grades."

Mum sighed. "I told you, Chantel, didn't I, you couldn't do this play and expect to keep up your schoolwork."

"Please, Mum. I'm so tired."

"I have to take off work tomorrow and go all the way in to have a conference with your principal. That really upsets me. I just want you to know."

"I'm sorry, Mum."

There was a loud sigh, and Mum shuffled back down the hallway. Chantel lay silent on the bed. In the darkness, I got up and closed the door.

"Is it true?" I whispered, switching the light back on.

"Is what true?"

"That you and the drama coach were caught fooling around?"

Her back was to me, but I could see it go rigid as a board.

"I guess the entire world knows."

"Mum and Daddy sure don't."

115

Suddenly, she turned and large tears were streaming down her face, smearing her makeup even more. It was the first time I'd ever seen Chantel cry.

"I'm in love, all right?" she said, struggling to keep control of her voice. "For the first time in my life, I've found somebody who cares about me, and I don't care what anybody says or thinks. Neither does he. He doesn't want to teach in that lousy high school anyway. We're going to New York together, and he's going to be a great actor some day. This place is a waste for both of us."

Stunned, I sat in silence. Finally, I asked, "Are you really going to leave?"

"I'm not staying here."

"Are you going to get married?" I was still trying to put the pieces together.

"Maybe."

"What about Mum and Daddy? What are you going to tell them?"

"Nothing."

"But you've *got* to tell them, Chantel."

She had stopped crying, and without even thinking about it, I went and sat on her bed. She sat down next to me and awkwardly held my hand for a minute. It was then I knew she really was leaving, but I couldn't think of anything more to say.

"You won't say anything, promise?" she said after a little while.

"I never do."

"I have to tell Mum and Daddy in my own way."

She got up and turned on the light in the closet. I watched in quiet awe as she brought a small suitcase down from the shelf and stuffed her clothes and things into it.

"Wish me luck, Evie," she said, fastening the buckles on her case. "I may not see you for a while, you know. They may try to find me, but I'm not coming back. Maybe you'll even come visit us someday." She bent down to kiss me. "Bye, Evie."

"Bye, Chantel."

"Don't hate me, Evie. I have to, you know."

"I know."

"It's just the way things happen in life sometimes. Someday you'll fall in love and you'll see, I hope."

Her last two words were so soft, more a sigh almost than words. The lights went out, and I felt her leave the room, the way she often had before, in the dark. But this time the darkness felt like the bottom of a deep, empty well.

In the morning, Mum came in to wake me up, but after snapping up the shade, she sat down on my bed.

"Evie, Chantel is gone," was all she said. Her voice was flat and faraway.

"What?" I said, sitting up and rubbing my eyes.

"Get dressed and we'll talk about it."

Calmly, too calmly, she walked out of the room and closed the door. I couldn't dress fast enough. Without bothering to wash my face or comb my hair, I dashed into the kitchen. Mum and Daddy were both sitting at the table, staring vacantly into their coffee cups. Daddy's face suddenly looked older and more wrinkled than I had ever seen it. A terrible pang of guilt shot through me.

Mum folded and unfolded a piece of paper. "She was gone when we got up."

"Did she leave a note?"

"Yes. She says she and the drama teacher are in love, and because the school and we won't permit it, she's going away with him." Mum's voice broke, and in her silent, reserved way, she bowed her head and cried.

Daddy shoved his coffee cup away and reached for his crossword puzzle. "I saw it coming," he grumbled. "Well, she'll never set foot in this house again. That's gratitude for you."

Mum cried even harder. "Please don't say that. I did the same thing when I was her exact age. I did the same thing, George. I ran away from home and married you, don't you see?"

"That was different. You were different. Everything was different," Daddy mumbled, gripping his pencil so hard that it suddenly snapped in two.

"How is it different? I hated home, and you cared for me. It's the same thing, George. We've made her hate us, and that's why she's left. If you wouldn't be so hard-hearted, so bitter . . ."

"Well, she's gone, and that's that," Daddy snapped.

"Daddy, don't talk to Mum like that," I ordered. I circled my arms around her and put my cheek down against her hair. She hadn't combed her hair either, and it stuck out all over her head. But it was soft and fine, and I lay my cheek in it as if it were a feathered nest to lay my troubles in.

I wanted to tell her how much Chantel had lied to her, that it was just the way Chantel was, and that I wouldn't ever leave her, even though I had in a way deceived her as well. But I was struck dumb with the revelation that Mum and Chantel were both the same person, and what Chantel was had begun a long time ago.

12

IT WAS strange that Chantel was gone, that I had my own room now and didn't have to wade through her pink bras and girdles in the bathroom anymore. She didn't leave much behind either except some stuffed animals—a pink elephant and a green alligator some guy had given her. Mum packed all her things in one box and stuck it on the shelf in the closet, and that was it. Chantel was gone.

I didn't miss her, and yet there was a dreadful quiet about the place that bothered me. Every once in a while I pulled the box down and went through it. I looked at the animals and her beauty notebook and odds and ends of cheap, castoff jewelry. Then I put it back again. It bothered me that Mum and Daddy didn't want to talk about her anymore. It bothered me we might never know what happened to her. She never wrote to say where she was or if she'd gotten married.

Mr. Herron never did play Rachmaninoff for me, nor did I ask him again. I bought a used record player at a garage sale and three different albums of Rachmaninoff. Now that Chantel was gone, I could listen to anything I chose for as long as I chose. I could read or just think and do nothing. It was strange at first, but peaceful, and the more peaceful it became, the less I felt bothered.

I made a vow not to sneak off on Mum, not after what Chantel had done. I made a vow to forget about Mike, even if I couldn't forget the music. But sometimes vows can be kept, sometimes they can't.

It seemed when you made a vow, you were supposed to do

something, like shave your head or not eat meat. That's what Bobby said the Catholics did. We didn't do anything like that in the Episcopalian church, so I decided to try something different and let my hair grow. I didn't cut it that winter or the next winter. I didn't think it would grow much, but it grew longer than Chantel's, not as thick, but with a shine like a sun-drenched glaze. It had a soft, autumn color to it, and I liked the feel of it blowing wildly about my shoulders up on Bracken's Hill.

I bloomed along with everything else on the island after those winters had passed. "Goodness, you've shot up like a weed, Evie!" Mum exclaimed.

"Fine, I'm tired of resembling a Chihuahua."

"You never resembled a Chihuahua."

"Thanks, Mum."

There was something proud in her eyes, and something of fear, too. "Not a weed," she said quickly, "but a rose. My Barbara Eve's become a rose."

The first warm day of spring, I rode my bike along the causeway. I liked the feel of the sea breeze whipping my hair behind me. I'd grow it to my toes, I decided. I would have the longest hair in the school.

Where the causeway joined the mainland, a small, green park jutted out over the beach and water. An art fair had been set up there, and people were milling about to inspect the paintings. I coasted through, admiring the stock seascapes and girls in floppy straw hats. And then I saw Mike.

He was much leaner than when I'd seen him last, his hair longer and bleached blonder as if he'd been spending a lot of time in the sun. His pottery gleamed under the spring sky in every brilliant color of the rainbow. But the purply-stone-colored pots still were the most beautiful.

I crashed into another biker before I could stop. The two of us tumbled over into the grass with a loud clatter, and immediately we were the center of attention. The other biker was swearing and grasping his knee. My own knees were gashed and burning along with my elbows, but I was too embarrassed to say a word.

Mike leaned over me along with a dozen other people. "Are you okay?" he asked, not recognizing me.

My heart was beating at a wild gallop. I couldn't look at him. The other biker had gotten up, but my own legs were too weak and wobbly to move.

"Are you okay?" Mike asked again. Everyone else was asking the same thing, but all I could hear was Mike's voice and the wild gallop of my heart. I flung back my tangled hair and made an effort to stand. But my legs wouldn't hold, and I sank down again in a helpless heap.

"She's okay, she's okay," I heard Mike saying. The biker was inquiring about me, and then I heard someone say something about calling an ambulance, and I found enough breath to gasp, "No!"

Mike took my hand and inspected my legs. "I think she's just a little stunned by it all," he said. "Does anything hurt?"

Nothing hurt. Everything was numb. I looked at him full in the face then and said, "I don't know, Mike."

He looked away as if he were going to say something to somebody; then a shine came into his eyes, something incredulous and wonderful, and he laughed. "Barbara Eve?"

His eyes were even crinklier at the corners, but still as bright and blue as his purest blue glaze. Dumbly, I nodded.

"I guess it's kind of a shock," I mumbled.

"Are you sure you're okay?"

"Yeah, I'm okay," I laughed, finally standing up.

He took my bike and led me, still wobbling, away from the crowd over to a rusty green van parked alongside the beach. He made me sit inside it while he went to wet some strips of cloth in the drinking fountain. Bathing my knees and elbows, he laughed again and again.

"This is unbelievable! How are you, Barbara Eve? I've missed your little visits. Beethoven and Mozart miss you, too."

I laughed, too, at him tying up my knees with his ridiculous bandaging. It felt so good to have the laughter back.

"I've missed you, too, Mike."

He looked at me with that puzzled expression of his as if he didn't know how to react or what to say. He fiddled some more with the bandages, tying them in bigger knots than before.

"I can't believe I didn't recognize you. Charm school must have paid off. You've grown your hair out. Or is it a wig?"

"Ugh!" I moaned, pretending to slug him.

"You've become quite a—" he said, ducking.

"Quite a what?"

"Quite, quite a lady."

"Yeah, I don't resemble a Chihuahua anymore."

He laughed. "A Chihuahua?"

A vendor trundling an ice cream cart stopped a few feet in front of us. "How about an ice cream?" Mike offered.

"Chocolate!" I responded with enthusiasm.

Mike came back with two ice cream bars, and I bit into mine eagerly, swinging my bandaged legs over the edge of the van.

"Think you can walk now?"

"I don't know. You tied these bandages too tight."

"I have to get back to my pottery. Come sit with me and tell me everything."

I walked stiff-legged with my bicycle back to Mike's exhibit. There were customers ready to buy, and plopping down in the grass, I watched him carefully wrap each piece in newspaper.

"Chantel ran off with her drama teacher, and we haven't heard from her since," I told him first. Then I told him about everything else, about school and how I hated the junior high, the gym clothes and the folk songs, about the strange, peaceful quiet Chantel had left behind, everything except the vow.

"You've stayed away too long, Barbara Eve," he said as I helped him pack up finally. It was twilight. "There's no one to help me clean anymore."

"It'll cost you this time," I teased back.

"I'm more than willing," he said with a smile. "Do come by if you ever can. Now hop in, and I'll give you a lift home."

I stared at him, panicking. "You can't do that, Mike. My mum and dad would both die of instant heart failure."

"But how will you get home?"

"On my bike, silly. I'm perfectly fine. Just loosen these bandages a little, okay?"

He tweaked my chin, and then with his bright smile, waved and chugged off in his van. I watched him go, forgetting I'd ever made any vow.

I never lied to Mum, not directly. But I suppose a lie is anything that isn't the complete truth. All I cared about was being with Mike, hearing his laughter again, and if that meant lying, then I didn't care what the consequences were.

I told Mum I wanted to stay after school once a week and take a pottery class if she could spare me from the store. That was the lie, and it wasn't a lie, for I was staying away *after* school, I said, not *at* school, and I was going to be working with the clay again. The part about Mike was more a secret than a deception, I told myself, and secrets belonged to nobody but yourself.

I caught the bus after school into Boston and found my way to Mike's shop, remembering every step of the way. The Common was still sprinkled with hippies and war protesters, hanging idly about in a park bursting with spring bloom. Antiwar posters seemed to have become a part of the background along with everything else.

Nothing had changed on Charles Street. The courtyard was still like a magic garden, sparkling with pottery, and the angel in the fountain smiled with the same amused smile at the spouting fish in his chubby arms. Mozart was sitting on the brick around the fountain, licking himself. He paused to look up at me and let me scratch his chin with a mild, contented roaring in his throat. *I have come home,* I thought, and yet at the door my heart took up its wild gallop again, and I had to lean against the doorpost.

He didn't see me but was busy at his wheel, his eyes and hands intent on a whirling mass of clay. I stood quietly watching him and listened to the music. It wasn't the Rachmaninoff but something silvery and playful, like a fish escaping with the bait.

I watched him until he finished his pot. After wiping off his hands, he looked up.

"Barbara Eve! You've come!" He hopped off his stool and came towards me, still wiping his hands on the clay-caked towel.

"What brings you to Boston?"

Alarmed at the continuing rush through my heart, I clung tightly to the doorpost and wouldn't move. "I told Mum I wanted to take a pottery class after school," I said sheepishly. "I guess I kind of told a lie."

"Kind of."

"Well, I didn't tell her any more than that, so she *thinks* I'm at school, but I never said I'd actually *be* at school."

"Which is still kind of a lie."

"Well, is a secret the same as a lie?"

"Not always. One shouldn't be disarmingly honest and open about everything. Some secrets should stay secrets. But you should always tell the truth. It makes life a lot less complicated in the long run."

"Well, if you should always tell the truth, then how can you keep a secret?"

"It all depends," he said, smiling and rolling out a new chunk of clay, "on what the secret is."

I finally let go of the doorpost and wandered slowly through the shop, taking in all the new pottery remembering every detail I'd forgotten. I came close to him and perched myself on a chair to watch the magic pyramid spring up from the shapeless clay. A giddiness ran through my body as I watched his hands.

"I like having a secret," I confided shyly. "I like being here and no one else knowing. Even if it is a lie not to tell Mum. But after what Chantel did, she'd never let me come if she knew." Something shuddered within me, so that looking full into his face, I quickly added, "And I just had to come, Mike. I'd forgotten how free I am being with you."

Mike reached out and touched my arm. It was as if a jolt of electricity zapped through me. "Barbara Eve, I want you to come visit. But I don't want you to get in trouble or hurt your mom and dad by getting it in your mind you're going off on a secret rendezvous like your sister. It's different, okay? Do you understand the difference?"

"Yes, I think so," I said shyly. "But I don't think they would."

"Maybe if you took them into your confidence, they would."

I shook my head vehemently. "You don't know my mum and dad, Mike."

I remained still, watching him and feeling a strange confusion. Something had happened, something was different.

"Do you remember anything I taught you?" he asked, grinning.

"I'm . . . I'm not sure."

He let me sit at the wheel with his perfect ball of clay. I remembered it all in my head but not my hands. The wheel's magic eluded me still, and my fragile pot went wobbling around like a flat tire.

Tears suddenly sprung from my eyes, and embarrassed, I wiped them away, leaving two smudges of clay across my cheeks.

"Hey, it's all right," Mike soothed, handing me a dirty towel. It didn't help except to make me laugh. He laughed, too.

"See, it takes time, doesn't it? You can't just walk away and come back and presto, you can make a pot! You have to grow along with it. It takes time to grow, Barbara Eve, remember?"

"It takes forever," I lamented.

"No, it doesn't. Believe me, it doesn't. Look how you've grown since the last time I saw you! Let's go."

"What?" I said, startled. He was heading for the door.

"Come on, let's get out of here."

"Where are we going?"

"Out. I have some errands to run."

He hung a BE BACK LATER sign on the door and took the stone steps two at a time. Incredulous and excited, I scrambled after him. He didn't slow his pace for me, but in long, swift strides took on Charles Street as if he owned it. His long, sun-streaked hair flowed out behind him, waving up and down as he walked. Everything that was free was Mike, doing what he pleased when he pleased, at the wheel with his pots or walking like this in the open sunlight with his hair flapping behind him. I ran breathlessly as if after a bird.

It was different and exhilarating to be going up one street and down the next with Mike, poking around in paint shops and hardware stores. Somehow it meant I was a part of his life now, not just the other way around. I could be close to him, walk with him, with nothing to distract his mind except his small purchases.

After the paint shops and hardware stores, Mike led the way into a junky, secondhand bookstore.

"What's in here?" I asked, wrinkling my nose at the musty smell of old, discarded books.

"A very special book," Mike said with an air of mystery. Intrigued, I followed him down one book-lined aisle, then another.

He crouched down in front of the bottom row of books and nimbly ran his fingers along their faded, raggedy spines. He frowned for a moment, as if it wasn't where it was supposed to be, and then broke into an ever-widening smile.

"Ahh, here it is!" he exclaimed, carefully extracting an ancient-looking book from the others. The jacket was nearly torn in two, and the pages threatened to crumble at any moment.

I almost laughed. "What is it?"

"The Beginning Potter," Mike said reverently. "This is the first book I ever read on pottery and still the best. Everything is written in the simplest terms, the way it should be. It's out of print, unfortunately. I found it here a couple of weeks ago, but since I already have a copy, I didn't buy it."

"So why are you buying it now?"

He handed it to me. "For you," he said simply.

"For me?" I was dumbfounded.

"Sorry it's not in mint condition, but I haven't seen it anywhere else."

"Oh, Mike, I'll treasure it always," I gushed. I turned to the first page. There was a big coffee splat on it and the inscription, "To Fred, Best wishes, Aunt Mildred."

"Who do you think Fred was?" I said, giggling.

Mike shrugged. "He obviously didn't give a hoot about pottery. Or Aunt Mildred. But don't worry, I'll fix that for you."

"No, I kind of like it this way, 'To Fred' and everything."

"Well, it's the book that counts."

"You can't judge a book by its cover!"

"Or by Fred."

Then we both laughed, so hard a customer came around to see what funny book we'd found.

"The Beginning Potter," Mike said, "you'll laugh your socks off! Come on, Fred. How'd you like an ice cream cone?"

"Serious?"

"I've never been more serious in my life."

Mike paid for the books, and then led me into the ice cream parlor next door.

"What'll it be?" he asked.

I stared indecisively into the creamy pink and chocolate craters underneath the glass counter. "Vanilla," I said.

"*Vanilla?* What kind of choice in life is that?"

"All right, fudge ripple."

"Fudge ripple, and make that a double. I'll take the strawberry cheesecake, double dip, please," he told the boy behind the counter. "Fred, let's live a little, what do you say?"

Fudge ripple never tasted so good. We stepped outside, licking up the dribbles running down the sides of our cones.

"Did you ever make a vow, Mike?" I asked.

"Once, in Viet Nam," he said, hesitantly.

"Did you keep it?"

A distant, almost sad expression came over his face. "It was more a bargain with God, really. You can't bargain with God and make a vow at the same time. A bargain has a condition on it; a vow doesn't, or shouldn't if it's made to God. That's what makes it binding."

He took a big bite out of his strawberry cheesecake and looked at me curiously. "This sounds serious. What kind of vow are you talking about?"

"Well," I said solemnly. "I can't tell you. But is it a very bad thing to break a vow?"

"No worse than lying when you've promised to tell the truth."

"What if you break a vow to God, would you go to hell?"

"Have you broken a vow to God?"

"Well, I didn't exactly make a vow *to* God, but whenever you make a vow, isn't He listening?"

"It depends on the vow, maybe."

I didn't know how to answer him without telling him. "When I'm with you, Mike, I believe in God," I said pointedly.

"That's a great compliment, Barbara Eve."

"So wouldn't it be better to believe in God than try to keep a vow you made when you weren't sure you did?"

Mike shook his head in amazement. "I wish I knew what you are talking about exactly. But I think I understand. It is better to believe, pure and free, without condition. But I don't think one is necessarily mutually exclusive from the other."

"Like what do you mean?"

"Well, if you vowed to never cheat on a test because you were afraid Someone or Something might zap you, and then came to believe that Someone was God, you couldn't think it was better to believe and cheat than not believe and not cheat. It would be pretty hypocritical, don't you think?"

"But what if the vow goes against something that's right?"

Mike stopped me in my tracks. "You're feeling pretty guilty, aren't you? Barbara Eve, I'm sure it's not irrevocable."

But it was, I wanted to tell him. When the laughter returns and you believe in God again, it's only the beginning of irrevocable.

13

I LOVED him for two years without telling him or without Mum knowing. How could I have told him or her or anyone that he was the air and the sea and life itself? He *was* my life, my only life in so many ways, like the sea, full of mystery and strength and vitality. I didn't think then that I could have lived my life without either of them, or loved anyone and anything more.

I poured my heart into the clay, for I had to pour it into something, and gradually I learned its secret. It was a secret of love and patience as well as control and determination that brought the walls of the pot up strong. Mike guided my hands and fingers until I understood, and then it was up to me to persist. I was in high school now and had access to a wheel and kiln in art class besides my visits with Mike. The art teacher thought I was something of a marvel. So did Mum.

I should have known Mum was not blind, except when she chose to be. Perhaps she knew all that time, after all, while I was growing more and more like a woman. Perhaps the pain of her life made her a keener observer than I knew. Perhaps love is a truth that won't stay hidden, no matter how hard you try. I think these were both true. But for all that time, Mum said nothing until she chose not to be blind anymore for fear of losing me, too.

"You can wash dirt off your face, Barbara Eve, but not your heart," was how she said it simply.

Her tall figure was silhouetted in my bedroom doorway. It was midnight, and I was sitting in my nightgown in the open window, humming Rachmaninoff's piano concerto. The sound of the sea washed gently in the night air, prickling my skin and hair and filling me with the indescribable.

"Mum!" I exclaimed, slipping off the sill. "What are you doing up?"

"Couldn't sleep, same as you. Mind if I come in and have a little chat?"

I leaned back into the shadow of the windowsill. Mum sat down on my bed in a filtered wreath of moonlight and clutched at her robe.

"There's a young man, isn't there?" she said, her voice faltering. Rubbing her cheeks, she gazed past me out the window.

I sat there, numb. "Why do you think that?" I said finally.

"Your moods, the way you eagerly run off and come back smiling, the light in your eyes . . . I made a promise not to pry, but I think that's been wrong of me. You've grown . . . so lovely, Evie. You're sixteen now. I feel as if I hardly know you. I don't doubt your integrity, so you must forgive me if I have compared you to Chantel. I know it's not fair. And yet, it has been on my mind for quite some time. A mother sometimes senses these things."

She waited for me to say something, but there was nothing I could give her. I continued to stare out the window.

"Forgive me, Evie," she tried again. "Maybe I'm wrong. But it's different with you than with Chantel. You're more than Chantel will ever be. Please don't deceive me, too. You have so much to give, Barbara Eve. Don't give it all away now. Perhaps I'm too late. I should have said it a long time ago."

"I haven't given anything away, Mum," I said softly. Unable to move, I felt as if the weight of everything would crush me and force out the words Mum wanted to hear. But it didn't, and I still couldn't say them.

Mum began weeping softly. In agony, I finally sat down next to her and held her hand. "*Please* don't cry, Mum," I pleaded, wrapping my arm around her thin shoulders and gently shaking her. "It's not what you think, I promise. Please don't. I hate what Chantel did to you. I'd never hurt you that way."

And yet I had in a way. Even more so, perhaps. But I couldn't tell her, not now.

"I'm sorry," Mum gasped, pulling a tissue out of the folds of her robe and blowing. "I've never really, well, talked to you about such things. It's my fault. But when two people truly love each other, they respect each other in every way. You're so young, Evie."

"Mum," I interrupted, not wanting to hear any more. "Mum, I'm not sleeping with some guy, okay?"

She turned and, taking my face in her hands, looked into my eyes with a sad kind of yearning. "All right, Barbara Eve. I won't say any more. But whenever you feel you can tell me, I want to listen, okay? Whatever it is."

"Thanks, Mum."

She kissed me, and then padded softly to the door and out of the room. I crawled back under the covers, stretching my arms through the pattern of moonlight and shadows. I lay awake, wondering if I would ever sleep. What was it like to really be loved by a man? I thought about it, playing with my hair on the pillow, until I decided I would wait a long time to find out and that it would be with only one man in my life. I decided it, not because of Mum, but because it was what I wanted.

The summer passed quickly, one day blending like mist into the next, like all the summers before. Mum kept her promise not to ask any more questions, but since she'd already guessed my secret, or most of it, her silence only added to my misery.

One Sunday afternoon, I sauntered, then broke into a sprint down the hill to the Cove, across the beach, and up Bracken's Hill. I spread myself across the flat rock that jutted out over the water and listened to my heart pumping vigorously within me.

When I finally sat up, I looked dizzily back across the Cove at our store. A large, rusty green van had pulled up outside it. Mike had a van like that.

Jumping up, I watched petrified as a man climbed out of the driver's side. He had dark hair and a dark beard. It wasn't Mike. Then a young woman with unmistakable long, chestnut hair emerged from the other door. My heart began pounding again, this time with dread and disbelief. I raced down the hill and back along the beach. By the time I reached the van, the couple had disappeared.

I took the back stairs two at a time, and then suddenly lost all my nerve. Pushing the door open as gently as possible, I sneaked into the kitchen on tiptoe. They were all in the living room. As soon as I came to the door, they saw me.

"Hi, Evie," Chantel said as if she'd just come home with her date. She looked tired and pale, but somehow prettier and softer. I realized it was because she wasn't wearing any makeup.

The dark-haired man was much older than Chantel. He stood with his hands in his pockets jingling keys as if ready to leave.

"Marty, this is my little sister, Evie," Chantel said, trying to sound cheery. "Only she's not so little anymore."

We stared at each other until I blurted uncomfortably, "What are you doing here?"

She frowned, as if hurt, then quickly forced another smile. "I wanted you all to meet Marty, Evie. We're . . . we're moving to California. A friend of Marty's is opening an acting school out there and wants Marty to teach in it. Isn't that exciting?"

Dumbfounded, I looked past her at Mum and Daddy. Mum's eyes were red, and she sat nervously twisting her handkerchief. Daddy stared coldly ahead, refusing to look at them and clearing his throat.

"So Mr. Peters, are you going to have the decency to marry my daughter?" Daddy said. "If you're here for any other reason, you can leave now."

Marty's face blushed bright crimson as he looked at the floor. "Mr. Cooper, uh, neither Chantel nor I believe, uh, that's right for us just now. We each need our freedom to be our own person. But we also love each other and want to be together. So we are doing what is best for both of us, and we felt that we ought to make amends with you, sir, if that's possible."

Daddy turned and jabbed his finger at him. "You know, both of you have a lot of nerve coming here. What kind of wimp are you, running off with a girl half your age? Do you know how her mother has suffered? Get out of here, and don't ever come back!"

"I'm sorry, sir, that you're entirely unable to love your daughter." Marty took Chantel's arm and moved her towards the door. "Let's go, Chantel."

Flustered, Chantel hesitated a moment before going with him. "I'm happy with my life. Doesn't anybody care?"

"Is he taking care of you, or are you taking care of him?" Daddy thundered. "Well, don't write home when you're broke and he leaves you, because you won't get one red cent, do you hear?" Mum ran after them while Daddy kept shouting. I watched him working himself into a frenzy, and for a moment it scared me. He leaned forward, straining every blood vessel in his face and neck, his eyes bulging so that any moment it seemed they would burst.

"Calm down, Daddy!" I yelled, surprised to hear the sound of my voice against his.

He glared at me. "And whose side are you on?"

"Nobody's."

I fled through the kitchen and out the door onto the landing. Mum was hugging Chantel next to the van.

"Now you send me an address this time so I can write to you," I could hear her saying. She was stuffing money into Chantel's hand.

Chantel looked up at me with a smile, suddenly full of hope and happiness, and waved. "Wish me luck, Evie," she called. "Someday I'll be a big star, and you'll all be proud you knew me."

I could only stand there and stare at her. She climbed back inside the van, and as they turned the corner, I watched her disappear out of my life for the second time. Stunned, I sat down on the top of the stairs and clasped my hands around my knees. Mum stood in the road for a few minutes, twisting her hanky. Then, slowly and breathing heavily, she came back up the stairs.

"Well, I . . . I hope she's happy. I . . . I'm really not so sure."

"Mum, why did you give her money? That's the only reason they came, you know. She knew you'd be soft."

Mum stopped in the middle of the stairs, her hand trembling on the rail. "At least they came."

"Oh, Mum, I'm sorry I said anything. Please don't cry." She plunked down on the step below me and threw her arm across my lap. I leaned over and hugged her neck.

"It's okay, Evie. It's . . . it's just . . . I suffer because I know she will suffer."

"Mum, I think you ought to quit feeling like it's all your fault. Let Chantel solve her own problems."

"It just hurts, Evie," Mum said, biting her lip. We sat quietly for a while, listening to the sea and the evening with its late summer sounds and breathless warmth. I somehow felt removed from it all, as if still watching from Bracken's Hill. It was like a dream, and Chantel had never been there at all.

"Well, I'd better go check on Daddy," Mum sighed. "He'll be wanting supper. What shall I fix?"

I shrugged, not wanting to go in. "I don't care. I'll come help you in a minute."

Mum sighed again. "He'll be unbearable tonight." Mum left me, only to rush back screaming. "Evie, come help me! Daddy can't breathe."

I jumped out of my reverie and raced inside. Daddy was still leaning from his chair, but this time he was clutching at his chest and gasping for breath.

"Call the fire station," Mum ordered. "Tell them it's a heart attack."

They were there with the oxygen in a matter of minutes. Daddy's face was white with pain, and he wouldn't let go of Mum. She held his hand as they put him on a stretcher and carried him down the stairs.

"Darling, you're going to be all right," Mum soothed. "It's going to be okay."

I had never heard Mum call Daddy "darling" before. I stared at her as if she were someone I didn't know, and then trotted desperately after her.

"I'm going, too!" I shouted, continuing right into the ambulance with Mum.

No one argued. We sped towards the mainland under the wail of the siren. Mum kept holding Daddy's hand while I scrunched my legs up in the corner and kept as still as I could, acutely aware of my own breathing and my own healthy, thumping heart.

"Chantel won't even know," Mum mumbled with a half-sob.

"Chantel!" I exclaimed. "How can you even think about her, Mum? If it weren't for her, Daddy would never have had this stinking, lousy heart attack!"

"But she won't even know she's hurt him. Or how much. I've no way to tell her."

"But you've got me, okay?" I wanted to scream. "*I'm* the one who's here. Not Chantel. Just me, Mum! Don't I count?"

I wanted to make another vow, that somehow I would make it all up to Mum. I didn't know how. That was the truth in me I didn't know yet.

14

I STARED at my reflection in the mirror with fierce determination. Then with a singular whack of Mum's sewing shears, sent my long hair tumbling in ribbons to the bathroom floor.

There. Absolved. Satisfied, I picked up the long strands of hair and braided them together. I no longer had a vow to keep. I would walk into Mike's shop one last time, and that would be the end of it. Mum needed me. Mike didn't.

Yes, it was better, I thought, feeling quite heroic. I would just tell Mike I couldn't come anymore, that Daddy was in the hospital, and Mum didn't need any extra worries. I couldn't lie to her, and that was the way things had to be.

I coiled my braided hair in a box to put on the shelf with Chantel's things. And after that, I didn't worry about truth-telling. Sooner or later, I'd find out what the truth was. For now, some things were best left on the shelf.

I walked into his shop with something more like giant moths than butterflies fluttering in my stomach. Mozart greeted me at the fountain with his usual indifference, but Beethoven sat up in the doorway and let out a quizzical *maoww?* as if unsure it was me.

Mike looked up with a perfectly blank face. Nothing was registering. He opened his mouth slightly as if to say something, but closed it again. Then I saw it was a matter of shock.

It was a few minutes before he said anything, and in those few minutes I wished an enormous hole would open between the two of us and swallow me up body and soul.

"You cut your hair," he said finally with a sad voice.

"Don't you like it?"

"Not on you. It's not, well, just not right, somehow." He came over and tried to steady my quivering chin. "I'm sorry, I shouldn't have said that. What is it, Barbara Eve?"

"Daddy's in the hospital," I told him, biting my lip and still not looking at him. "Chantel showed up with Marty out of the clear blue, and Daddy had a heart attack."

"I'm so sorry. How is he?"

"He's fine. Mum's friend, Sylvia, runs the store for her so Mum can spend most of the day with him. It's been real hard on Mum. The reason I cut my hair is because I broke my vow and because I can't come here anymore."

"What vow, Barbara Eve?"

"The reason I grew my hair long in the first place was because I made a vow."

I looked up then to see if he was laughing. But he wasn't. His eyes were dark and serious.

"Is it okay to tell me now what sort of vow you've been trying to keep?" he asked.

It wasn't what I'd planned, not at all. I felt like a total fool. But I couldn't escape the truth I was seeing reflected in his wonderful face.

"I made a vow two years ago I'd never sneak behind Mum's back," I said. There was such a tight feeling in my throat that the words barely squeaked out.

"And for two years, longer than that, that's what you've been doing," he said, or I thought he said. Perhaps only his face, not his voice, said it.

"But I haven't done anything wrong! I'm not Chantel!" I exploded, my voice precariously on the edge of tears.

"Of course, you're not, and that's the problem, or rather that's why it's a problem. You can't bear a lie."

"I couldn't help it, Mike! Mum would never allow it, not after what Chantel did and now nearly killing Daddy on top of it."

Then I said it. It rang out like the blast of a foghorn echoing off every gleamingly polished curve of every pot in the studio, blasting the truth in full force into Mike's face and bouncing back into my own.

"I'm in love with you!"

I'm in love with you. It sounded as foolish and wrong as Patricia Lamont's pink School of Beauty, the words fluttering in front of me like a pair of glued-on eyelashes. That wasn't how they'd sounded when I'd thought them, not on dark nights listening to Rachmaninoff.

I'm in love with you. I remembered then that I'd tied my hair back in a long, sweeping ponytail and chopped it off as if chopping off an arm or a leg. Now I was standing there in a crazy, hack job of a hairdo, feeling twelve years old again. Only this time the Rachmaninoff wasn't playing, and I couldn't take my hair off.

Mike's face hadn't changed. It was still solemn and all-knowing. The half-amused, half-puzzled look wasn't there at all. If it had been, I don't think I could have taken it. As it was, something desperate already had happened, and like the waves rushing against the purply stones, he neither rejected it nor accepted it. He simply let it be. It wasn't a lie, but it wasn't truth either.

I couldn't stay after that. I turned and fled from his presence, nearly tripping over Beethoven in the doorway. My legs felt awkward and uncoordinated as if somehow they had turned into brittle sticks that could no longer hold me up. I stumbled up the steps, then on the bricks in the sidewalk, and all with the sickening knowledge that I could never return again.

I took off towards the opposite end of Charles Street that met the river. I didn't look behind me or turn to look in any shop window. When I finally reached the river, it wasn't clear in my head what I meant to do there. What I ever meant to do or be again seemed as dark and remote as the depths of the river itself.

I finally collapsed on the grassy bank, and tucking my knees up under my chin, watched the sailboats and Harvard crew teams glide by like figures in a dream.

I didn't know he'd followed me. When I looked up to see him standing there, tall and graceful as the willows, my mind went blank. The grass, the river, the boats, all blending in perfect harmony around me—how had I gotten here?

"Why did you run off?"

"I don't know."

"Can we talk about it?"

"I've made a real twit out of myself this time, haven't I?"

"A what?"

"A twit. You know, an idiot."

He sat down and stretched his long legs to meet the river. Pulling up a long blade of grass, he began sucking on it. "I don't think you're a twit," he said. "A lot of things are happening to you, Barbara Eve, a lot of things you need to talk about."

"That was a twit thing to say though," I answered, my voice trembling.

"That you're in love with me?"

I nodded helplessly, keenly aware again of the sudden disappearance of my hair and entire self-respect.

"That wasn't a twit thing to say, Barbara Eve, not coming from you."

"Yes, it was. Why should I have said it? You're not in love with me. I never thought you were. Now it's spoiled everything."

"No, I'm glad you said it. It's time you said it. Now we can go on."

"How?" I said miserably.

"As the good friends we really are."

He pulled me into his arms then, close, holding me against his heart, so that in between the sobs, I could hear its steady beating. It was all I wanted in life, to be held there in the strength of his arms, safe against the life-pulsing force in him always.

"Someday you will say those words to someone, and they will be right. You'll know it, and he'll know it. But give yourself time, Barbara Eve. You're just beginning, remember? It's the same as becoming a potter. Real love can happen in an instant, like a good pot, but the potter has to be trained and ready for it."

"I'll never love anyone but you, Mike," I sobbed all over again.

"Yes, you will. And it will be a very beautiful and right thing, as will the vow you make."

When I walked into Cooper's Grocery Store late that afternoon, the little silver bells that jangled over my head seemed to be heralding the arrival of something new. It was a quiet jangling, nothing loud and prolonged that would disturb anybody, just enough to catch someone's notice, to say a door has opened.

Mum had returned and was busy with a customer, but she took the time to look up as she always did.

"Barbara Eve Cooper, whatever have you done with your hair!" she gasped.

"I cut it."

"But why? It was beautiful." She turned back to her customer. "Sorry. My daughter has just given me a dreadful shock."

I wandered behind the counter and began fixing two teas while Mum finished counting out the woman's change. I hadn't noticed about Mum. Maybe it was the way the evening sun was mixing shadow and light across her face, or maybe it was this new thing inside me, but for the first time I saw that her hair was going gray. Her skin was flaking, but worse than usual, so that her face and hands looked nearly crimson. Daddy was, and always had been old, but Mum was becoming old.

She smiled and said, "Thank you," the polite way she always did. Then the bells jangled again once, and it was quiet.

"Evie, where on earth have you been?"

"I had something important to do today, and never mind my hair. It'll grow. How's Daddy?"

"As good as can be expected."

"Tea, Mum?"

"Thank you, Evie." She looked at me expectantly.

"Mum," I said, taking a deep breath. "Mum, I have something to tell you. There's more than just a pottery class."

Mum didn't say anything. She paused slightly as if a speck of dirt were floating around in her tea, and then raised the rim of the cup to her lips.

"I've been learning pottery," I continued slowly, bending my face into the comforting steam from my teacup, "but not at school the way you've been thinking. The way I wanted you to think."

Mum kept sipping her tea, one tiny sip after the other until I saw she still wasn't going to say anything. It was up to me to say what I had to say first.

"I've been going into Boston," I told her. "When Chantel and I were taking that charm class, Miss Lamont embarrassed me so badly, I had to get out of there. She treated us like a bunch of poodles. So I ran off and discovered this pottery shop on Charles Street where all the art galleries and antique shops are. This potter there makes the most beautiful pottery I've ever seen. He said he'd teach me for helping him clean his shop. So that's what I did while Chantel took poodle lessons. But then he became my friend, the best friend I've ever had. He makes me laugh and listens to me and teaches me things. Like telling the truth. Only he's never pushed me to it.

"But I guess I didn't really want to know what the truth was. Because I was afraid after Chantel left that you'd never trust me, you'd never allow it. So I've been lying to you really, even though I didn't want to admit it. But now I'm telling you because I learned something new today, and it means you have to trust me because I can't be a liar anymore, but I also need Mike to be my friend. And that's all it is, a close friendship."

Mum set her cup down and finally turned to look at me. Her eyes were moist, but she didn't cry. She just looked at me the way I'd wanted her to look at me when the bells jangled and I stepped inside The Coop with my hair whacked off.

"Thank you, Evie," she said in a whisper that ended in a sad, little laugh. "I'm not at all sure what else to say or think at the moment."

"Just let me know it's okay, Mum."

We took to each other's arms then, the way two people do when one has crossed an ocean to meet the other.

15

"EVIE, I want to go to Boston with you," Mum said. She was serious.

"Oh, Mum! It would mean so much!" I had been begging and pleading with her to come meet Mike. To see his shop. Just once. I jumped up from the kitchen table and threw my arms around her neck.

She smiled tiredly and patted my arm. It was late. "I pray about my cares and troubles so much. For once, I want to forget about them. I want to meet this potter."

Mum decided to wear her blue suit she only wore for special occasions. It was a soft gray-blue color that matched her eyes and made them shine. She had a little blue felt hat that had a bit of black ribbon on it, and she covered up her hands with white gloves. She looked hopelessly outdated, but to me she was beautiful.

"How do I look?" she asked anxiously.

"Gorgeous, Mum," I said, giving her a kiss.

"We're going to Boston," Mum told Daddy uneasily. "Just for the afternoon. Sylvia will be in the store."

"Boston?" Daddy said with a blank stare. "Boston?"

"Yes, dear," Mum said, giving him a quick kiss. "We'll be back before you know it."

We took the bus, and Mum nervously grasped her handbag the entire trip. "I hope he'll be all right," she fretted.

"He'll be fine, Mum," I assured her.

"You must try to love your father a little, Evie," Mum said.

I sighed. It wasn't what I wanted to talk about.

"Whether you feel it or not, Evie, you need to try a little. He won't live much longer."

It was something Mum had never said before. I didn't look at her because I knew it was a hard thing. I wished she hadn't said it.

"I'll try, Mum," I promised.

"You came all this way?" she said, amazed as I led her from the bus stop past the Boston Common and the Public Gardens to Charles Street.

"It's not so far, Mum."

"Yes, it is far," she said as if thinking of something else.

We came to the little sunken courtyard and the angel in the fountain, and I tried to picture it as Mum would, having never seen it before. She stopped and gasped at the brilliant array of pots. Then she read the brightly lettered sign aloud, THE CHARLES STREET POTTERY.

We moved carefully down the steps and into Mike's shop. As usual, Mike was sitting at his wheel, deep in concentration. Mum blinked, adjusting her eyes to the dusty light. Something lively was playing in the background. Mozart perhaps.

"That's Mike," I whispered to Mum, watching intently for her reaction. It wasn't disappointment, but it wasn't pleasure either. She hadn't decided yet. She took in the cluttered shop, his shabby clothes, the beard, the rough hands, but nothing came back. She seemed to be waiting for something to happen.

Suddenly, I wasn't so sure about the whole idea. What if it all went wrong and Mum wasn't impressed? I smiled at the sight of Mike's shining hair flowing freely about his face and thought, after all, what more could I do or say?

"Hello, Mike," I said at last when he looked up at us. "This is my mum."

His eyes widened in surprise, and he stood up. "Well, what an honor, Mrs. Cooper. I—uh—sorry about the hands," he laughed, uselessly wiping them on a dirty towel, reaching for Mum's neatly gloved hand, then quickly withdrawing his again.

Mum laughed nervously. "How nice to meet you, Mike. Evie has finally told me all about you."

He looked at me and winked. "Good things, I hope."

"She can't say enough good things."

"Your daughter is becoming an excellent potter."

"She's had an excellent teacher," Mum said, her gaze finally settling on a row of Mike's brilliant blue teapots. "Your work is beautiful."

"Why, thank you."

She silently caressed each pot, and as she turned toward me, I knew she believed me.

"It's . . . it's really beautiful pottery," she said with awe in her voice. "I've never seen anything quite like it, although I don't know much about pottery, of course. I guess I've always thought of it as being rather dull and earthy, the colors, I mean. I've never seen such brilliant colors, really, the blue especially."

"The blue is Mike's specialty," I explained, feeling my own excitement growing. "It reminds me of the colors of the purply stones on the beach."

"The purply stones?"

"The little stones I'd bring back from the beach. These colors remind me of them, all wet and glistening. Only the stones would fade. But these glazes never will."

Mike threw another lump of clay on the wheel. We stood and watched his hands swiftly shape it into a round bowl.

"It's amazing, isn't it, Mum?" I murmured.

"And this is what comes of it," Mum said, admiring the teapots again. "I'd like to buy one of your teapots."

"It's yours," Mike offered. "A gift."

"Oh, no, really! I must pay you for it."

"Not when it's a gift."

"But, really!"

"Really!"

I smiled proudly at Mike as he carefully wrapped the teapot in newspaper for Mum. He playfully shook my shoulder. "Thanks for bringing your mother in, Barbara Eve."

"Thank you, Mike."

"Really, this is too kind of you," Mum said.

"Not at all, Mrs. Cooper. Thank you for coming."

Mum smiled thoughtfully back at him. "Thank you, Mike."

He stood at the door as we left. At the top of the steps, a sudden gust of wind snatched Mum's hat clear off her head and sent it tumbling down Charles Street. Mike and I were after it in a flash, but it was Mike who caught it, leaping out in the street and grabbing it in midair like a Frisbee. As he waved his catch high over his head, his laughter rang out for all of Charles Street to hear.

I turned in astonishment. The wind was blowing Mum's hair and skirt as well, and she was laughing too. Mike handed her the hat with a touch of ceremony. Still laughing, Mum stared at it as if it were a flying saucer. "Thank you," she said breathlessly.

A lightness enveloped us both as we watched him go.

"So thoughtful," Mum said on our bus ride home. All her nervousness was gone. She sat quietly looking out the window. "Your father was like that once, you know. He used to bring me cakes and jam when I first met him, and sugar being so scarce during the war and all. Little things like that meant so much."

"Why did he have to change?"

"He's a proud man, your father. To not be in control of your life or your household, that kind of thing devastates a man."

"It's devastated us too, Mum," I answered quickly, feeling the anger rise in me again.

"Yes, it has, Evie. But that's what you have to let go of. That's what you have to understand."

We got off the bus and stood waiting for it to rumble ahead. The sky overhead was a pale, delicate blue, and we both stood with our chins tilted, as if to drink in its promise of freedom. Mum seemed reluctant to move after the bus and its explosive exhaust had cleared out of the way. She was smiling, and her skin had lost its redness. For a moment, there was almost a luminous quality about it, something reflecting the clarity of the sky above us.

"You've made a wonderful friend, Evie," Mum said softly. "And I'm glad he's been your friend. I was your age exactly when I met your father, and he was several years older. I know that happy feeling I see in your eyes. I know what it means. So do you understand how I should feel about all this?"

"He's never taken advantage of me, Mum."

"I believe that. But a lesser man would."

We crossed the street then, without hurry. The luminous moment had passed.

"He's full of such joy, Mum," I tried to explain.

"And that is why you love him," she said matter-of-factly. "And why I'm afraid you'll be hurt."

"We've dealt with that already, Mum, and it's okay."

"Things change in every relationship, Evie. Someday Mike may not be there for you. That's what I mean."

Like Daddy, like the whales. Like sometimes the feeling that God wasn't even there, and you had to make the long, lonely journey by yourself. But that wasn't true. God *was* always there. Maybe that joyous love that came out of people like Mike was a guiding star to tell you He was. It takes a special inside feeling like that to be able to travel great distances.

We showed Daddy the teapot. He knew nothing about Mike, nor did he need to. My interest in pottery meant little to him.

"Can't make a living out of it."

"I'd like to be a *teacher*, Daddy. I'd like to teach science and art, and pottery on the side."

"Teaching don't pay much either."

"What do you want me to do? Rob banks?"

"Evie's talking about going to college, dear," Mum said patiently.

"College? Sure, and turn into one of them drug-crazed hippies."

Exasperated, I gave up. How did Mum go on loving such a man? Because he once brought her cake and jam? Or perhaps because the laughter had once been in him, too, before I could remember. I didn't think she really hoped to hear it in him again. She loved him because it had been there, but beyond that, she was as helpless as he was in knowing how to bring it back.

She left me alone with him one night. Sylvia, our new clerk, was in the hospital having bunion surgery, and Mum had gone with Sylvia's husband to visit her.

"Her whole face looks like a bunion. She should have it removed."

"Daddy, that's not a very nice thing to say about Sylvia," I countered. "She's been very good to Mum."

He mumbled something else incoherent, and then stared dazedly again at his television program. I was at the kitchen table, trying to work through an algebra problem. Outside, a storm was brewing. The wind was rattling the windowpanes, and I could hear the trees lashing against the back side of the house. Thunder rumbled in the distance, then cracked like a gunshot almost overhead. Soon rain was pelting the roof and windows with increasing gusts of fury.

Then, suddenly, the lights went out.

"Evie!" Daddy called out at once.

"I'm here, Daddy," I called back, fumbling around in the kitchen drawers for candles.

"Evie!" he called again, but this time it was in a low, almost frightened moan.

"I'm coming, Daddy. I'm trying to find candles."

"Evie!"

I found Mum's Christmas candles and a couple of candle holders stashed in the back of a cupboard and quickly lit two of the candles.

"I'm coming, Daddy," I said, bringing the wavering tokens of light into the pitch-black room. They made an eerie glow, and the terrified look they illuminated on Daddy's face sickened me. He could have been a ghost.

"Daddy, are you okay?" I cried, quickly setting the candles down on a table.

He didn't say anything, but clutched my arm so hard it hurt.

"Daddy, let me go check the fuse box," I said, firmly extracting my arm from his grip.

"No, no, don't leave me," he pleaded, almost like a child.

"Daddy, I'm just going to see if I can get the lights back on."

The fuse box was in the coat closet. I held the candle close enough for light and tried to trip the switch, but couldn't.

"Looks like we're stuck in the dark, Daddy," I sighed.

"Evie!" he moaned again. "Can't breathe."

"Daddy, let me go get your medicine," I said. *Daddy, don't die on me,* I panicked to myself, taking a candle into the bathroom and searching for his medicine. "Please, God, don't let him die on me."

My hands were trembling so hard I couldn't open the bottle. "Okay, Eve, cool it, he's not going to die, he's not going to die." The cap flew off, and half the pills went flying, too, across the bathroom floor. "Later, Eve, just bring Daddy the pills in your hand."

"Here, Daddy, take these," I commanded, lifting a glass of water to his lips. "Drink the water. Drink the water, Daddy!"

"Evie!" he moaned again.

"Daddy, you're going to be all right!"

He clutched at me again, and the fear in his face was unlike any I had ever seen. "Daddy, it's the storm. It'll be okay."

"They're out there," he said in a frozen whisper.

"Nobody's out there, Daddy. It's the storm."

"They're out there. You can't see them, but they're out there."

"Who, Daddy?" Now I was beginning to feel frightened.

"The enemy. They've got us covered. Stay down in the fox-hole."

"Daddy, this isn't a foxhole! I'm Evie, your daughter, and we're right here in our living room!"

Daddy had never lost his mind before. I wanted to run out and cry for help, but I was too afraid of leaving him. I bumped my way back into the kitchen to the telephone. It was dead, too. In desperation, I stumbled into my bedroom for my flashlight. Holding tightly onto Daddy, I began flashing an S.O.S. signal out the window.

"I'm calling for help, Daddy," I said.

"That's good, that's good. But keep low."

I don't remember how long we sat there like that, my holding him and his clutching on to me for dear life, or so it seemed, or how long I flashed my signal. My arm ached, then went numb, and the light kept flashing anyhow. I didn't know and never will know what light snapped off in Daddy and what light suddenly flared up in me. I only knew for the first time his fear and how it had affected his life, not from any war, but from still living while dying. I had never understood it. I hadn't known how.

"I love you, Daddy," I soothed him over and over again. "I love you."

Suddenly, there was a pounding on the door and a voice saying they'd seen my S.O.S. signal. Some kid had taught it to a school class in the Cove one year, and how could you forget a thing like that?

"I love you, Daddy." It saved his life for a little while, and that was all I clearly remembered.

16

CHANTEL didn't come for Daddy's funeral. She has never come back and probably never will. It was just me and Mum, a few neighbors, and Mike, who had never met Daddy.

He was buried in the same little cemetery where Bobby's father was buried. Only there were no military people, no gun salute, even though he had been a soldier himself, and his gravestone would say so. He'd succumbed to a different kind of war, a war he couldn't fight, and now the quiet said it was over. Viet Nam was over, too, or so they said. The men would be coming home now. It was a war we couldn't fight anymore.

I went up to Bracken's Hill often. The dinghy had been taken over by two small boys. They had patched and painted it, figuring it had long been abandoned, which it had. I felt ashamed and would not repossess it. It was enough to watch them shouting and laughing as they tested their droplines for tinker mackerels and then gallantly threw them back. *Sorry for the inconvenience!*

It was enough to listen to the sound of the purply stones and to think of my future. I wanted to teach, and I wanted to live on the mainland. I would leave the island and Musk Cove.

Mum changed, too, in ways. The redness went out of her skin altogether, and she began to laugh. But the island was all she knew. She would stay.

On Sundays, I went with her regularly to the little stone Episcopalian church. It had a large rose window in the front on which Jesus was ascending to heaven. I sometimes imagined He looked at me.

And Mike came to the island for visits. He had a way of dropping in unexpectedly, but Mum was always glad to see him because she loved him, too. He talked about moving to New Hampshire to the country. That was his dream, and I couldn't begrudge it.

Then in the spring, life changed again. Mum had said it would. But that I didn't foresee. Mike and a strange girl both hopped out of his van at the same time. He was wearing his usual painter pants and t-shirt. She was petite and dark-haired and wearing a billowing Indian smock and leather thongs. As she moved closer to the store window, the more distinct and beautiful her face became. It was a curious mix of something natural and delicate and exotic as a flower. With an uncertain stab of fear, I thought how interesting they looked together.

Mike saw me through the door and waved. There was a special excitement in his face I had never seen before. Mum hung back while I opened the door.

"Mike!" I shouted it like a cheerleader.

"Barbara Eve!" he shouted back.

Then he took my hand and gently moved the girl towards me. "I'd like you to meet someone."

I knew before he said it. Something went reeling helter-skelter inside of me.

"This is Helen Chen. I wanted you to be the first to know. Helen and I are to be married."

Helen gave me her hand and smiled. She had dimples, one in each cheek. I couldn't take my eyes off her. *No wonder*, I thought.

"You must be Eve," she said in a musical kind of voice. "Mike's little sister."

"We met several weeks ago at an art fair," Mike explained. "Helen is quite an accomplished artist. We're going to be married this weekend. Neither of us wants a big wedding. Then we're going to New Hampshire and start looking for a house." He laughed as if he couldn't quite believe it. "I wanted you to know. It's so sudden and everything, *I'm* still in shock."

Mum came forward then to congratulate them and invite

Jean Harmeling

them to stay for a cup of tea. But no, they couldn't stay. They had a lot to do before the weekend.

Mike hugged me and gave me a tender look that said, *Be happy for me, Barbara Eve.*

We stood at the curb and waved good-bye. Mike blasted his horn, and we waved again. Then the van was gone as quickly as it had appeared.

I stood motionless for a long time, it seemed. Mum quietly put her arm around me and walked me upstairs. She let me cry for a good while, and then pulled my head up and wiped away my tears.

"It's a big shock, isn't it?" she said. I nodded through my tears. "Even when you knew it wasn't right, you still had this dream he'd wait for you."

"I'll never love anybody else, Mum. Not ever."

"Well, forever's a long time, don't you think?" I was thinking that didn't matter, that life would go on, that . . .

"Barbara Eve Cooper, I know what you're thinking," Mum said, looking sternly into my face. "Mike has his life to live, and you have yours. Now, let's go out, what do you say? Dinner and a movie? My treat."

"Okay," I agreed reluctantly. "Mum, do you think you'll ever get married again?"

"I don't think so," she said simply. "I'm a bit used up. But you, you're just beginning."

Someone else had said that to me. Then I remembered it was Mike.

I don't know how it became clear to me. On an impulse, I think. I decided to paint Mum's awning, so I marched into Ralph's Hardware and marched out again with two buckets of candy-apple red, brushes, scrapers, stirring sticks, thinner, and assorted pans. I lugged them out of the store and then dropped the brushes and pans and sticks all in the middle of the sidewalk.

I set the paint cans down, but I didn't pick up the brushes and sticks. I was at the top of the hill, and there was The Coop with its shabby green awning and door. And at the bottom of the hill was the Cove where the water was sparkling today with tiny starbursts everywhere. There were the boats in the marina and the two Morris boys dragging their dinghy out to fish. I could hear the gull crying *screee* and the sound of the waves rushing towards shore. I could imagine the silver gleam of the mackerel just below the surface of the water, a hidden treasure from the deep.

And suddenly I knew what it was I had in me as if it, too, were gleaming silver just below the surface. "I will choose to love," I decided. That had been Mum's choice. And Nita's. And Mr. Hughes's. And Mike's. And God's. That would be my choice, too, whatever it meant.

I picked up the brushes and sticks and paint cans again and jangled my way through the front door of The Coop.

"I think it's time we paint this place," I explained. "You always talk about it and never do it."

"Oh, Evie!" Mum laughed and tried to say something else. But all that came out was, "Oh, Evie!"

And I laughed with her. When something becomes finally clear in your mind, the laughter will come close behind. Was that what Mike knew? It was what he'd taught me.

I put on my scrubbiest t-shirt and jeans and began scraping away at the faded green paint on the awning and door. In a day's time, I gave The Coop a whole new outlook on life. The brilliant red paint transformed the drab storefront into something alive again.

"Do you think it's *too* red?" Mum asked doubtfully.

"Mum, it looks great!"

Then she smiled and laughed heartily. "Evie, it's outrageous, don't you think?"

I stood back whistling, hardly conscious I was doing so because it all felt so good, the vibrancy of the red paint under the bold blue sky, along with this new feeling inside of me. I even tried whistling Rachmaninoff until another whistle, coming from somewhere, brought a different tune in altogether.

I stopped and looked up. A few feet away stood a boy with

dark hair that had a cowlick and flopped in his eyes. He stopped whistling and smiled, at once familiar and yet a stranger. He was no longer a boy, really. He'd grown tall.

"Hi, I'm looking for Eve Cooper," he said with mischief in his eyes.

"I'm Eve Cooper," I answered like an idiot. The mischief didn't go away.

"Don't you know me?"

"Bobby?" I was thunderstruck.

"It's been a long time, hasn't it?"

I stared at him, thinking how handsome and like his dad he'd become and wondering what miracle had brought him back to Musk Cove.

"I'm here with my mom and Bill and Teeny," he said, reading my thoughts. "They're still down at the cemetery. It looks like I'll be coming back to Boston. I'm starting at Harvard this fall. I skipped a grade." He sounded embarrassed to say it. All these years. He hadn't written a word.

"How are you, Eve? I'm afraid I haven't been a very good corresponder. I hope we're still friends."

I looked down self-consciously at my paint-smeared jeans and t-shirt. At least my hair had grown out again. The breeze wisped it softly against my face. Was he noticing?

His smile was the same, boyish and sincere, and still a little shy. I could feel the blood rushing to my head and pounding at my temples like mighty gongs. It was then I remembered what seemed another lifetime.

"Welcome back." I opened out my arms to embrace him.

He laughed, as if he too remembered. There was no shyness in him now. His arms were warm and tight and unafraid.